Dead End

There Are No Good Guys

By Jerry Bader

MRPwebmedia.com/books

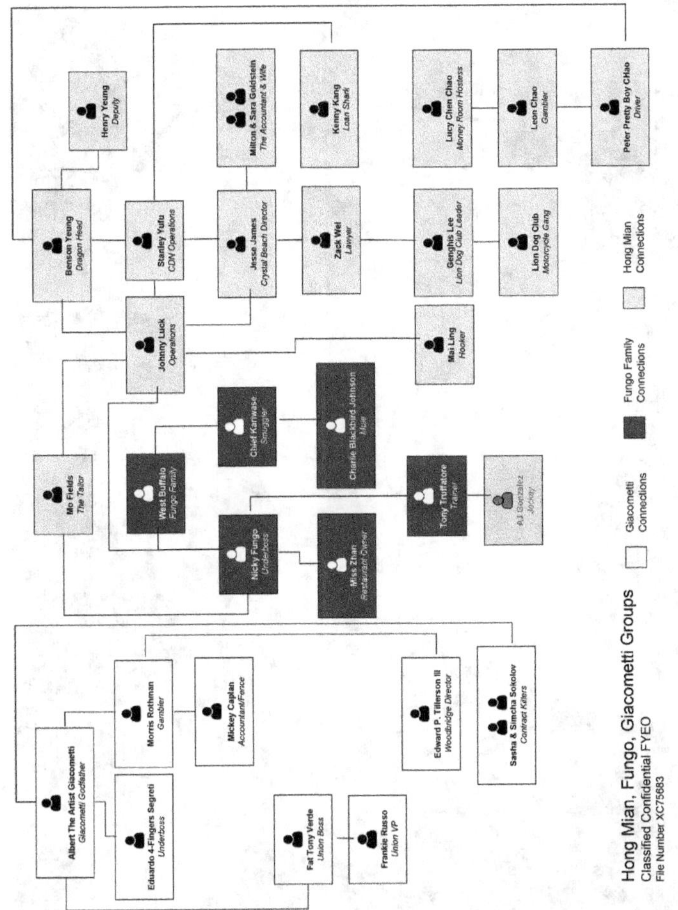

Hong Mian, Fungo, Giacometti Groups
Classified Confidential FYEO
File Number XC75683

HONG MIAN, FUNGO, GIACOMETTI GROUPS

THE GIFT

I
The Gift

Five Years Earlier,
Beverly Hills Shopping District, Rodeo Drive

A large black limousine pulls up and parks under the "No Parking Anytime" sign in front of the Three Kings tailor shop. A beat cop on his rounds notices the car but keeps on walking past as if it's invisible. In the front seat is a driver dressed in a black suit, white shirt, and black tie with a Guan Yu stickpin. In the back is Benson Yeung, an elderly Chinese gentlemen, wearing a beautiful, charcoal pinstripe bespoke suit, a crisp white shirt, red silk tie, and a Guan Yu stickpin.

The driver gets out of the car buttoning his jacket to hide the Smith & Wesson Bodyguard® 380. He proceeds to the rear passenger door and opens it. The elderly white-haired man slowly exits the automobile carrying a black ebony cane with a gold dragon's head handle in one hand, and a small shiny red bag overflowing with gold tissue paper in the other.

The two men enter the Three Kings. It's a well-appointed shop with bolts of expensive fabric lining the walls, and mahogany wood paneling displaying numerous Hirschfeld-style caricatures of famous clients. Mo Fields, the owner, is seated at a large mahogany partner's desk at the far end of the showroom doing paper work; his six-year-old daughter Betty is seated opposite reading Roald Dahl's 'The BFG.'

Betty turns to see who's entered. As soon as she realizes who it is, she jumps up and runs to the old man, clutching his well-tailored leg as if it was a prize possession. Her father smiles at his daughter's reaction. He gets up to greet the old man. The little girl notices the red bag and points. She blurts out, "For me?"

The old man smiles, "Patience little one, patience..." He goes to hand the little girl the bag but stops. "Do not open it until I tell you. Understand?"

The little girl bobs her head up and down.

"Now go and read your book, while I talk to your Father."

The little girl snatches the red bag from the old man and hurries back to the desk with her mysterious package. Too excited to read, she just stares at the bag as if staring will reveal its contents.

The driver moves to the door scanning the street for anything that looks suspicious.

Fields and the old man move off to one side as if they're selecting fabric for a new suit. The old man takes a photograph of four men out of his jacket pocket and points to the one man who's Chinese. "That one. Tonight."

Fields takes the photograph and looks at it carefully, imprinting the man's face in his memory. "What about the others?"

"Just the one, he's the *Pantu*… the traitor. The others are *Shagua*… fools."

The others are a grossly overweight fat man in a grey three-piece suit, a bug-eyed fop with a white silk puff hankie overflowing the pocket of his tuxedo, and a creepy little thug wearing a shabby suit and a Borsalino that all but covers his face.

Fields nods and hands the photograph back to the old man who slips it back into his pocket. He takes his hand out of his pocket holding a stickpin in the shape of a Blue Chinese Lantern. "Make sure you wear this."

Mo Fields understands the significance of receiving the Blue Lantern. Only Chinese can wear the Guan Yu pin signifying membership in the Hong Mian, the most powerful triad in North America with connections that spread from Hong Kong to LA. Only trusted non Chinese associates can earn the Blue Lantern status, making Mo Fields one of the trusted few.

Fields acknowledges the instructions and takes the talisman. The old man turns to see the little girl looking intently at the red bag. She senses his conversation with her father is finished and turns to look.

Finished with his business the old Chinese gangster turns to the little blonde daughter of the tailor. "Now little one, your patience is rewarded."

The little girl grabs the red package pulling what seems like an endless supply of gold tissue paper from the bag. She reaches in and pulls out a brightly painted statue of a fierce looking Chinese warrior. The eight-inch figure has a red face, long beard, and green robe wrapping around ornate body armor. He's carrying a long-handled weapon with a crescent-bladed battle-axe spewing from the mouth of a jade-headed dragon. The statue makes an odd clinking sound as if partially filled with pebbles as the little girl waves her new prized possession in the air.

"It's beautiful Uncle!" She calls him Uncle out of respect and love.

The old man smiles at the delight of the little girl. "You keep this on your desk for good luck. Guan Yu will protect you, so keep him close. Understand?"

"Yes Uncle I understand, I love him. I'll call him Red Face. How do you say Red Face in Chinese?

"His name is Guan Yu, but you can call him *Mian Chi*, Red Face. Now go and pick out a nice fabric for me."

The little girl jumps from her chair and runs to a shelf holding bolts of the most expensive Vicuna fabric in the shop. Her father laughs. The old man turns to Fields... "You've taught her well. Make one charcoal and one black. And don't forget the surgeon's cuffs."

Betty carefully places the statue on the desk. She imagines a time when the exotic warrior with the red face lived, and wonders what kind of adventures he must have experienced. The old man finishes his business with the tailor, kisses the little girl on the head and leaves.

THE HIT

II
The Hit

Mo Fields walks into the Green Dragon Restaurant. The Dragon is safe territory controlled by Benson Yeung and his Hong Mian Gang. It's Friday night, and the place is hopping with an assortment of Chinese gangsters, movie executives, and the occasional misplaced civilian.

An odd group of misfits are sitting at a table situated next to the entrance to the kitchen. Four men occupy the table: a fat man overflowing his three-piece suit as he ostentatiously pats the sweat from his brow; a vaguely effeminate dandy with bulging eyes in a dark suit with a white silk hankie spilling out of his breast pocket; a scruffy gunsel who doesn't bother to remove his oversized fedora; and a thirty-something Chinese man in a trendy suit and spiked hair.

A beautiful young Chinese woman with an expensive Vidal Sassoon haircut approaches Fields. Sally Yang is as exotic as she is beautiful. She wears a long high-necked, gold silk cheongsam with a green dragon wrapping gracefully around her breasts and backside. The dress features a teasingly sensual slit up the side, almost to her hip, revealing a long lovely leg balanced on a shiny green spiked high heel.

"Good evening, sir. A table for one?"

Working for Benson Yeung taught Yang to pay attention to details like the working cuffs on the man's suit jacket: a sartorial refinement that denoted a well-heeled man of good taste. Fields raises his hand as if to wipe an imaginary piece of lint from his jacket. The woman immediately spots the Blue Lantern stickpin in his lapel.

"I'm meeting some friends."

Yang bows gracefully allowing him to pass. Fields quickly spots his man at a table strategically placed near the entrance to the kitchen. He reaches into his jacket for the Glock 30S as he briskly walks toward the table. The target is sitting with his back to the wall. As he passes the table he slows, just long enough for the man to notice, he raises the Glock and pulls the trigger. BANG!

A bright red hole appears in Peter Pretty Boy Chen's forehead; his brains are splattered all over the gold and green wallpaper.

Fields doesn't stop but keeps on moving out the door, through the crowded steamy kitchen with a dozen Chinese cooks all yelling at each other in Cantonese. Fields exits the back door, gets into the stolen car provided for him by Benson Yeung's driver, and disappears into the night before anyone in the restaurant understands exactly what has happened. It's all over in less than three minutes.

CHARLIE BLACKBIRD JOHNSON

1.
Charlie Blackbird Johnson

Present Day

Charlie Blackbird Johnson waits for his turn at the Peace Bridge border crossing. As a Native it should be a simple matter of flashing his Status Card. His band has been smuggling cigarettes across the border for years without much trouble despite the occasional gum flapping by the police and politicians worried about losing their tobacco industry campaign contributions. But this was a new enterprise. It wasn't cigarettes being brought into the country; it was ecstasy being sent out.

It was a simple job really. All he had to do was cross the border and drive to the Fashion Outlet Mall on Military Trail in Niagara Falls, NY where he would leave the car for the Italians. They'd pick it up, take it to a garage, unload the four kilos of ecstasy, and return it to the mall parking lot while Charlie enjoyed a nice steak and a few cold beers.

But Charlie Johnson was nobody's fool, or so he thought. He wasn't muling no Chinese dope to the Italians without easy access to some protection. Fuck the Chief and his no weapon policy. And why couldn't the band make the ecstasy? Why did they need the Chinese and the Italians? What was that all about?

Nicky Fungo and his old school goombahs with their Tony Soprano imitations were a joke. At twenty-one, Charlie Blackbird Johnson was smarter than all those dummies. It was a new world, and it was only a matter of time before his generation took over, and when they did, it would be Natives only, none of this multicultural cooperation bullshit.

Johnson drives up to the booth with his Status Card ready. The guard enters the license plate number of Charlie's Mustang into his computer. He turns, "Reason for visiting the US today?"

Johnson hands the border guard his Status Card, "I don't need a reason." The guard gives Johnson a hard look. This wasn't the first time he had to deal with a hard-ass Indian that thumbed his nose at border security. The guard holds his temper, chances are this jerk has a record, and that would make his day. He enters the identification information into the computer, and sure enough, Charlie Blackbird Johnson has a sheet: car theft, break-and-enter, and drunk and disorderly. Mostly smalltime stuff, but enough to give this prick a hard time.

"Mr. Johnson, your Status Card is only valid to cross the border if you have a clean record. And I see you've been rather a bad boy."

"This is bullshit! I'm entitled to cross the damn border anytime I want."

"Only if you have a Secure Certificate of Indian Status. Do you have one of those Mr. Johnson?

"I left it at home."

"I see... are you bringing any plants, firearms, or drugs into the US?

"No."

"Please pop your trunk and get out of your vehicle."

The ecstasy was hidden in the fender of the Ford Mustang. Unless this bureaucratic border prick decided to dismantle the whole car he was clear, but the Smith & Wesson M&P9 under the driver's seat and the Kriss Vector Gen II 9mm stashed in the spare tire compartment would be easy to find. Charlie Blackbird Johnson should have listened to the Chief, but Charlie was smarter than anybody he knew, certainly smarter than this border booth jockey.

There was no way he was going to jail. He rams his foot hard on the accelerator. The Mustang leaps forward crashing through the barrier, the force of the impact was harder than Charlie expected. Pieces of the barrier hit the windshield causing Charlie to lose control of the vehicle just long enough for the border guard to empty his government-issue automatic into the back window of the muscle car. Three of the slugs hit their target: one in the back of Charlie's skull, one in his neck, and another in his shoulder.

Within minutes, twenty border guards and Buffalo Police surround the Mustang, all with guns drawn. The ranking USBP (United States Border Patrol) officer approaches the Mustang and opens the driver side door. Charlie falls out onto the pavement, dead.

Charlie Blackbird Johnson wasn't quite as smart as he thought.

THE PLAN

2.
The Plan

Ex jockey, Jesse James, was still getting used to her new job as Director of Racing Operations at the Crystal Beach Racetrack and Entertainment Complex. After the accident at the Hancock in LA, Jesse knew her racing days were numbered. An ongoing feud with fellow jockey, Avellino Jose Gonzalez, culminated with Gonzalez driving Jesse and Good Night Sammy, a leading four-year-old money winner, through the infield fence of the Hancock Racetrack. Jesse had a broken arm, concussion, and various other internal injuries. It took months for her to recover fully, but Good Night Sammy wasn't so lucky. He had to be put-down. Gonzalez received a five-year suspension but Jesse's racing days were over. She was too valuable a Hong Mian asset to get killed on the track, besides, her mentor Johnny Luck had bigger plans for his pretty blonde protégé with the smart mouth and brains to match. Johnny promised Jesse that Gonzalez would be dealt with in due course, a suspension was fine, but a more terminal solution was required. A message had to be sent: you don't fuck with the Hong Mian.

Johnny's boss, Benson Yeung, is the Dragon Head of the Hong Mian. If anyone asked, the organization is merely a social club existing for the sole purpose of helping the less fortunate members of Chinese communities throughout North America. No one would argue that Benson Yeung, businessman and philanthropist, wasn't always ready to provide financial support for those less fortunate, however; one could counter that Benson Yeung ran one of the largest criminal enterprises in the United States, with tentacles that stretched to Hong Kong, Shanghai, Mexico, Colombia, and Canada. The Canadian operation is headed by Stanley Yufu, an impressive, elegant man in his mid forties with a remarkable resemblance to Jack Palance, if Jack Palance was Chinese. Yufu is a Toronto businessman that owns Green Dragon Stables and the Yufu Chinese Restaurant chain.

The Crystal Beach Racetrack was dying. The provincial government, on the urging of the Racing Commission, conspired to kill horse racing in out-of-town jurisdictions. Why would they do that? As it happens, the Racing Commission board members are the same establishment horse owners and political contributors that control the Woodbridge Downs Racing & Entertainment Complex in suburban Toronto, and they are determined to control the dwindling interest in pari-mutuel gambling.

Racetracks need slot machines to survive. Blackjack, poker, baccarat, roulette, and other casino style games are gravy, but slot machines are a must. By restricting slot machines to the Woodbridge Racetrack, the Commission all but guaranteed the death of smaller Southern Ontario racetracks. The value of horse racing facilities in Crystal Beach, Hamilton, Barrie, and several other ex-urban areas plummeted. But as the Chinese are fond of saying 'where there is danger, there is opportunity.'

Skyrocketing Toronto real estate prices push potential homeowners and businesses further and further out of town, thus creating the potential to profit from legitimate real estate investments. Friendly, mostly desperate, small town politicians fall over themselves attempting to attract new investment and jobs to their towns. Of course they'd prefer investment from good old Anglo Saxon stock, after-all, they aren't multicultural Toronto with its big city liberal notions. But in the end money talks, and with enough cash in play, even narrow-minded parochial politicians are prepared to turn a blind eye to some of the more questionable businesses being installed by strange people with funny sounding names. Nobody cares, as long as the money, jobs, and taxes keep rolling in.

Stanley Yufu, Johnny Luck, Benson Yeung, and Nicky The Mushroom Fungo create YLYF Entertainment Corporation to take control of as many Ontario racetracks as possible. Cash businesses like racetracks provide the volume vehicle needed to clean the large amounts of cash generated from the sale of ecstasy manufactured in Yufu's small fortunate cookie factories located in small towns. The product is distributed throughout the province by The Yufu Chinese Restaurant and Fortunate Cookie Company, and in New York, New Jersey, and Pennsylvania, by the expanding network of Fungo Pizza Parlors.

YLYF purchased the moribund Crystal Beach Racetrack, upgraded the facilities, and instituted big money stake races irrespective of the Racing Commission's efforts to limit Crystal Beach to only four racing days a week.

Despite losing race days, the big money stake races attracted better horses and more of them. As anticipated, the gamblers turned out attracted by the big money races and the big name horses. The earnings from the betting public were supplemented by a money-laundering scheme developed by Jesse's accountant, Milton Goldstein.

The previously rundown resort-town was fast becoming the place for young singles in Southern Ontario and Upstate New York to party, with Stanly Yufu supplying the party favors, available on special order from the new Yufu Chinese Food Emporium, conveniently located between the racetrack and the beach. If you weren't able to get to Crystal Beach for the weekend, you could call the Yufu takeout hotline and order some Scooby Snacks, Disco Biscuits, or Molly along with your Kung Po Shrimp and General Tso chicken. Special order fortune cookies with more than a fortune inside were a particularly popular item.

And if you were stuck in Upstate New York for the weekend, your fill of MDMA could be supplied by calling the local Fungo Family Pizzeria. Unfortunately supply was limited this weekend as delivery boy, Charlie Blackbird Johnson, was delayed by a terminal case of lead poisoning.

Jesse surveyed her new office that overlooked the refurbished Crystal Beach Racetrack. The large twenty-by-twenty-four photograph of Jesse on Medicine Hat that appeared in the LA Times, and the equally sized image of her and Medicine Hat in the Winner's Circle at Louisville Downs hung just above the walnut pedestal displaying Frederick Remington's The Outlaw, a gift from her mentor Johnny Luck.

Jesse is the Hong Mian's man, or rather woman, in charge of the Crystal Beach Racing operation. Jesse knows horses, racing, and how the Hong Mian does business. Johnny and Benson allowed Jesse to bring her father's old accountant, Milton Goldstein. Luck knew Goldstein well from when he dealt with Jesse's father, the late, unlamented Wally Nuts. With Johnny's approval, Benson agreed to the hire with the proviso Zack Wei was made Jesse's assistant. Wei is a small man of undetermined age; he could have been thirty or sixty, it is impossible to tell. He shaved his head, wore John Lennon granny glasses, and the obligatory expensive black suit with a Guan Yu pin ever-present in the lapel.

Wei is a lawyer with an interesting background. As a youth he was leader of a Chinese motorcycle gang called the Lion Dogs that distributed drugs in LA and Toronto for the Hong Mian. Benson Yeung recognized the young tough guy wasn't your average street punk. He plucked Wei out of the street environment and sent him back to school to become a lawyer. Wei's combination of street and book smarts made him an ideal Hong Mian executive. Up until recently he was Stanly Yufu's consigliere and bodyguard. Now he preformed the same duties for Jesse.

Milton and his wife Sara were reluctant to come
north across the border, but now they loved it.
The sleazy underworld action combined with the
youthful partying spirit of the town were just the
ticket for a couple of bored retirees looking to be
relevant again and not caring about the moral or
legal aspects of their golden years' adventure.
Jesse and the youthful chaos of the border
boomtown was just what they needed.

Milton walks into Jesse's office and drops the
morning edition of the Toronto Star on her desk.
Jesse scans the headline:

"Shootout At The Peace Bridge
Niagara Falls Native, Charlie Blackbird Johnson,
Killed In An Attempt To Smuggle Ecstasy Into the US."

Jesse looks up at Milton, "I guess it's time to think
about a Plan B."

THE GOLDSTEIN PLAN

3.
The Goldstein Plan

Jesse calls a meeting at Jimmy's Waterside Restaurant: a modest seafood joint with a great view of the canal and an owner that understands discretion. Jesse, Goldstein, Wei, and Yufu enjoy a nice lunch while watching the ships feel their way through the canal with only inches of clearance on either side. Over coffee the conversation turns serious. Jesse turns to Goldstein, "Milton, layout your plan for Stanly and Zack."

Milton drains the last bit of coffee from his cup. A white-aproned waiter appears with a carafe of fresh coffee in-hand. Stanly turns to the water and snaps, "Out!" The waiter leaves. Milton focuses in on Yufu and begins. "What's easier, picking winners or losers?" Yufu looks at Goldstein with more than a slight bit of annoyance. "Obviously losers."

Goldstein's leans forward with his co-conspirators following suit. "This is the beauty of this scheme. All we have to do is pick one or two losers in each race. We don't even have to fix the races, in fact, if some asshole starts fixing racings we have to deal with him. This whole scheme is legal... well except for the dirty money part."

Yufu becomes interested. "Explain... give me details."

"Okay, here's how it works. The first thing we do is form *The Thoroughbred Investment Corporation*. I'll come back to why in a minute.

We use the Pick 3, so we have to pick the winners of three races in a row, but if we bet on every horse in the race we're guaranteed to win but we don't have to bet on every horse. Say there are ten horses in a race. One or two are going to be outright dogs, so we eliminate them and we bet one dollar on each of the other horses. Let's say we only eliminate one out of ten horses in each race that's a twenty-seven dollar investment, but we don't just buy one ticket, we buy ten, so now we've invested two-hundred-and-seventy dollars per Pick 3. On a ten race card we can pull this off eight times.

So every shill needs two-thousand-one-hundred-and-sixty dollars to bet. Two buses of fifty ringers each, equals an investment of two-hundred-and-sixteen-thousand dollars. If the favorite wins every race at let's say three-to-one odds, we get back two-hundred-and-forty-thousand dollars per day. But of course we know that favorites only win about thirty-five percent of the time, which means the actual return will be much higher. Based on our current forty-day racing schedule we can clean eight-million, six-hundred-thousand dollars. Normally there is a cost to cleaning funds but with this scheme we'll actually make an extra nine-hundred-and-sixty-thousand dollars. That gives us an operational cash flow of nine point six million bucks. And the beauty is its tax free, clean, and legal... well almost legal, except for the dirty money part."

Yufu thinks for a second, "But the money technically belongs to the shills, not us."

"That's where *The Thoroughbred Investment Corporation* comes in. When the shills turn over the money, we get them to sign a contract with TIC to manage their investment in a string of racehorses that TIC purchases and manages. The shills technically own the horses and we, or one of our associates, administers the operation. As we all know, owning racehorses is almost always a losing proposition. As the management company we get to charge expenses, including a commission for purchasing the horses, a management fee for running the company including office staff and accounting, plus maintenance of the horses including the trainer, blacksmith, veterinarian, feed, barn fees, entry fees, and on and on. By the time we're finished, the shill's investment will get chewed up in expenses. TIC then sells the horses to recoup the losses and pay the management company - us. In the end all the funds end up in our hands, all nice and clean.

Yufu looks at Wei, the lawyer, "What do you think?"

Wei takes off his granny glasses and polishes them with the linen napkin as he speaks "My first impression is it's brilliant, but on reflection, I have to say..." He pauses for a moment, replaces the glasses back on his head, and looks up at Yufu. "It's fucking brilliant."

Everyone is silent absorbing the impact of the plan. Goldstein breaks the silence, "We can't get greedy and try to do too much; that's what creates red flags. If the system works at Crystal, we can expand it to Hamilton, Barrie, and a bunch of the other small tracks we've been buying."

After a couple more hours of discussion the plan is finalized. Busloads of paid shills from all over the province and Upstate New York would be brought in to clean the ecstasy money proceeds. Elderly Chinese retirees from Toronto and their Italian counterparts from Upstate New York would each be given fifty dollars spending money for lunch, two-thousand-and-sixteen dollars cash, and a racing form with all the Pick 3 bets marked. The shills would cash the winning tickets with the winnings collected by pretty hostesses accompanied by beefy uniformed drivers before they were allowed back on the buses home.

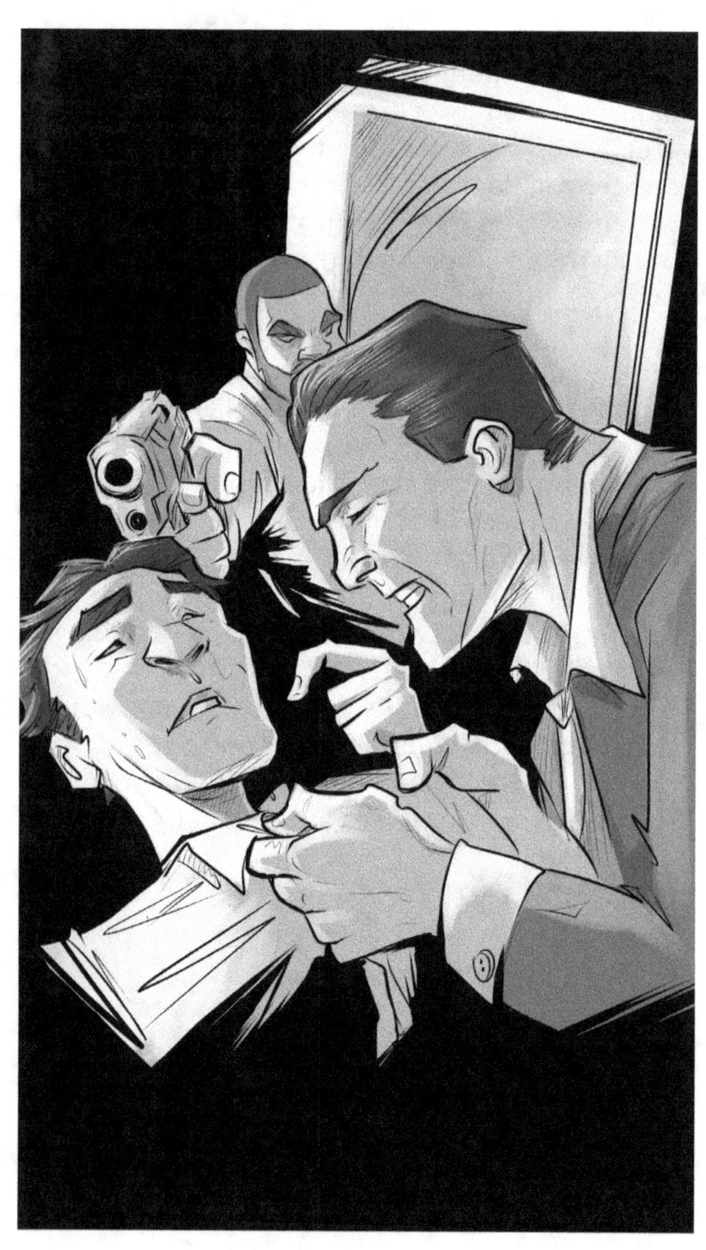

LEON CHAO

4.
Leon Chao

Leon Chao is uncomfortable. He squirms on the grey metal folding chair; the kind reserved for school auditoriums and group support meetings. A church basement would be a welcome alternative to what Leon expected the next hour would bring. Poor Leon made the mistake of borrowing money from Kenny Kang, a Hong Mian loan shark.

The room is large and empty, a warehouse probably, somewhere near the Distillery District. There are curious stains on the floor and walls that look a lot like dried blood, but perhaps that's just Leon's vivid imagination running amok. The room is cold and damp but Leon is nevertheless perspiring. He can't help it. He knows what's coming and it would probably end with more red stains on the concrete floor.

Kenny Kang stands silently in front of Leon casually smoking a Nanjing cigarette, one of the most expensive Chinese brands you can buy despite being associated with corruption, something Kang thought was à propos for someone in his profession. By Kang's reckoning, expensive meant success, and besides, it was better than smoking Zhonghua, a brand associated with Chairman Mao.

At the far end of the warehouse there's a large dented metal door that opens to a loading platform. Beside the dented corrugated steel is a wooden door that exits to stairs that lead to the parking lot. Two burly but well dressed Chinese thugs stand arms crossed over their black custom-made suits. If you're Hong Mian, you dressed like Hong Mian, and that meant expensive black suits. If you were high enough up the food chain, you got to wear charcoal or dark blue, maybe with a pinstripe, but never chalks stripes or windowpanes. Leave that shit for the Italians; they liked that flamboyant look, but not if you were Guan Yu, Hong Mian.

The door opens. A tall elegantly dressed Chinese gentlemen with more than a passing resemblance to Jack Palance walks in. He's wearing a dark blue bespoke suit of the finest Vitale Barberis Canonico wool, a crisp white Egyptian cotton shirt, and a red silk tie held in place by his Guan Yu stickpin. Leon knows exactly who it is. Stanley Yufu is Hong Mian's number one operator in Canada.

According to the RCMP, FBI, and Interpol, Yufu is on the same level as Johnny Luck in Los Angeles. Only the Dragon Head, Benson Yeung, and his eldest son Henry, AKA the Little Dragon, rank higher than Yufu. Even Benson Yeung's youngest son, King, the black sheep of the family, rated little more than grunt status after he was dishonored as a result of a failed art forgery scheme. Yufu walks to where Leon is sitting and stands off to the side not saying a word.

"You know who this is?" asks Kang.

Leon looks at Yufu and then back at Kang, "Yes, I know who it is." Leon knows better than to mention his name.

"So, here's the situation Leon, you owe us fifty-seven thousand dollars and we need you to pay it now."

"I can't, I don't have it."

Kang scratches the back of head as if he really doesn't quite understand Leon's respond. "You don't have it? Is that what you're telling me Leon? Cause if that's what you're telling me, it creates a problem."

"I can get, it will just take some time."

Kang raises his hand and with a flick of the wrist motions one of the thugs to come forward. The thug stands beside Leon's chair facing him with his arms down by his side. Leon looks up at the thug then back at Kang. Leon can smell the foul stench of fear permeating from under his arms.

The thug removes his Glock 37 Semi-Automatic from its shoulder holster and places it tight up against Leon's head.

"Time, Leon, is the enemy of us all. So tell me, do you think we're stupid?"

"Of course not Kenny…"

"While… then why are you treating us like we're stupid?"

"I'm not!"

Kenny doing a passable Chinese imitation of Samuel L. Jackson: "Oh but you are Leon, you're treating us like we're a bunch of dumb stupid bitches you can screw and not pay. And I don't like being treated like a dumb bitch." Kenny looks at the thug holding the gun. "Do you think Leon here, is treating us like a bunch of dumb stupid bitches?" The thug nods in the affirmative. "See Leon, it's not just me. We all think the same thing."

"It's been a rough few months, things will turn around, I can feel it."

"I don't think so Leon, you're a degenerate gambler and as soon as you lay your hands on some cash you'll find a way to blow it on the ponies at Woodbridge, you don't even frequent our nice new facility."

"It's in Crystal Beach for Christ sake. It would take me an hour and a half to get there."

"You got a phone Leon, You could call one of our associates who'd place your bets. You know we're a full service operation."

Yufu still hasn't moved or said a word.

"Okay, Leon I'm going to give you a choice. We can write the whole damn thing off, or you can do us a favor while you pay back every fucking cent you owe us, plus interest of course."

"That will take forever…"

"True Leon, very true. To be brutally honest, you'll probably never get out from under, but then again the other option is forever as well."

"I don't understand."

"We write off your debt Leon, we have to send a message to other deadbeats. And that message is really a dead end for you."

"So what do I have to do?"

Stanley Yufu has heard enough, Leon Chao, his brother Arthur, and his aging mother and father would be on the first Shanghai Racing Tour Bus headed to Crystal Beach where they'd receive a pocket full of cash and a Racing Form with all the bets marked. Of course none of them will ever see a cent from those bets, but they will get to keep the fifty dollars lunch money, if they don't blow it betting on their own selections.

LUCY CHEN CHAO

5.
Lucy Chen Chao

The Chao family wasn't happy with Leon, nor was his brother pleased about taking two-days off work every week in order to keep Leon from becoming a permanent resident of the Mount Pleasant Cemetery. They weren't happy, but neither did they want any trouble with the local Hong Mian. Leon's brother Arthur was particularly annoyed, a fifty dollar lunch spiff didn't make up for the money he would lose installing quartz kitchen countertops and backsplashes. Arthur was a good son, and he didn't want his parents to worry about something happening to Leon, so he kept his mouth shut and didn't say a word except to his wife Lucy.

Arthur loved Lucy, but ever since they met she seemed perpetually distracted. She had the odd habit of continually looking over her shoulder as if she expected someone was about to put a knife in her back. Her caution was well founded.

Lucy Chao was born Lucy Chen in Los Angeles. Her brother Peter worked for the Green Dragon Restaurant owned and operated by Benson Yeung. Peter was a good-looking Chinese hipster with big money dreams. He was always looking for shortcuts to making it big. Unfortunately, the Hong Mian doesn't work that way; you serve an apprenticeship, pay your dues, and if you're lucky, in time, you get to wear the Guan Yu, or if you're like Peter Pretty Boy Chen, you remain a lowly driver, ferrying senior members around town when not delivering sweet and sour chicken balls and fried rice to LA's trendier neighborhoods.

Peter got involved with the exotic beauty, Sally Yang, who was night hostess at the Green Dragon Restaurant. Like Peter, Sally had her eyes on the big score that led her to become involved with a crew of grifters intent on stealing the legendary ruby-filled Guan Yu statute that Benson Yeung was rumored to keep in his office.

According to legend, whoever possessed the ancient ruby-filled relic was entitled to be the Dragon Head of the Hong Mian. Whether the ancient artifact actually existed or not remains a mystery, but what is known is Benson Yeung became Dragon Head by employing a brilliant tactical mind, an accountant's flair for figures, and the ruthlessness warrior skills of the organization's patron warrior God, Guan Yu. This confluence of circumstance led to Peter Pretty Boy Chen's brain matter being splattered all over the dragon inspired mural that covered the walls of the Green Dragon Restaurant.

So when Lucy Chen Chao listened to her husband complain about the consequences to the family caused by his ne'er-do-well brother, she listened carefully. Arthur was so upset he didn't notice that his young wife's perpetual preoccupation had disappeared. She was focused on Arthur's every word. When Arthur ran out of gas complaining, Lucy affectionately kissed him on the forehead, made him some tea, and promised to look for a job to help with the loss of income.

It wasn't until later that night in bed beside her husband that she formulated her revenge. Her brother was a dumb ass, but he didn't deserve to die, and besides, she was tired of looking over her shoulder. The Hong Mian had a habit of eliminating loose ends, and Lucy Chen Chao was a very loose end. You did not want to be the sister of someone who tried to rob Benson Yeung.

Yufu's loan shark operation led by Kenny Kang quickly spread the word amongst delinquent customers that signing up for the weekly Shanghai Bus tours to Crystal Beach Racetrack wasn't an option. If you had a retired elderly parent you were encouraged to add them to the list. It wasn't quite a demand, but it sure seemed like one to most debtors. And if you had a pretty daughter or wife interested in being a tour hostess all the better. Lucy Chao was one of the first to put her name on the list.

JESSE'S PLAN "B"

6.
Jesse's Plan "B"

Nicky The Mushroom Fungo's idea of using Chief Kariwase's cigarette smuggling network to move the ecstasy across the border seemed like a perfect idea when he proposed it. Unfortunately, Charlie Blackbird Johnson's recent permanent retirement made that scheme impossible to continue. The USBP would be super vigilant targeting Natives for special scrutiny. The Chief could yell and scream about profiling all he wanted, but Homeland Security couldn't care less about human rights and hundred-and-fifty-year-old treaties. A new plan was needed. In Jesse's words, "It was time for a Plan B."

Jesse and Yufu were taking a tour of shed row with Zack Wei hanging back just in case a problem arose. Jesse hadn't quite got used to being shadowed by the quiet and rumored dangerous Zackary Wei. She still wasn't sure if he was her bodyguard or keeper. As with most things Hong Mian, the answer was probably both. As far as she was concerned, all she really needed for protection was the pearl-handled switchblade she kept tucked safely in her stylish black Cuban-heeled boot.

They stopped at one of the stalls where one of Yufu's broodmare's was having the Caslick procedure done in preparation for transport to a farm in Kentucky. The Caslick involves surgically sewing shut the opening of a filly's vulva in order to protect it from inflection. The Caslick is a sixty-year-old procedure developed by E. A. Caslick, DVM to prevent what is commonly referred to as wind-sucking or more correctly pneumovagina, where dirt carrying bacteria enters the animal causing inflammation of the vagina, cervix, and uterus, often leading to sterility.

Jesse touches Yufu's arm, "I think I might have a solution to our problem."

Yufu, still watching the procedure asks, "Which problem is that?"

"The logistics problem."

Yufu turns to Jesse. She's got his attention. "The Caslick... that's how we move the merchandise."

"You mean in the broodmare?"

"Yup... I bet we can get at least a kilo in there."

Yufu pauses to think for a minute, "A kilo eh? That's one million milligrams, about five thousand pieces at thirty-five bucks each retail, or about one-hundred-and seventy-five-thousand dollars per horse, per trip. We move a couple of horses a week from a half-a-dozen friendly owners that need working capital, and we're talking real volume. Shit… they could even send the horses back stuffed with powder. This could work."

Jesse looks up at the Chinese Jack Palance, "Well… I guess we got our Plan B."

ONE PLAN TOO MANY

7.
One Plan Too Many

Jesse's plan to move the drugs and Goldstein's plan to launder the money weren't the only plans in play. Lucy Chen Chao also had a plan. It was not as complex or profitable as Jesse's or Goldstein's, but she figured she could skim at least a couple of hundred thousand dollars over the forty-day racing season. It didn't make up for the murder of her brother, Peter, but it did help ease the pain just a bit. It's not that she didn't have concerns about getting caught, she did, but she figured by the time accounting caught the discrepancy, she and Arthur would be long gone. With cash in hand they could get a fresh start some place else, maybe Rio or Buenos Aires. Anyplace where the Hong Mian wouldn't find them. Besides, she always wanted to learn Spanish, and the winters in South America had to be better than Southern Ontario. As far as she was concerned, her deadbeat brother-in-law, Leon, was on his own.

The plan was simple: steal small amounts of cash from a lot of people over a long period. She figured nobody would notice. There was so much cash changing hands anything could happen. If they caught it, it could be chalked up to a couple of dummies that didn't follow instructions. That would be an easy sell, most of the old Chinese and Italians didn't speak much English, anyway. What were they going to do, bump off some old immigrant lady because she screwed up and lost fifty bucks? That would never happen, at least, that's how Lucy Chen Chao rationalized her plan.

Each bettor was supposed to receive an envelope of cash covering the bets to be made, plus fifty bucks spending money for lunch or whatever they chose to spend it on. Most people would probably blow it betting on losers. Lucy was the designated money hostess; as such, she was responsible for parceling out the cash to all the shills when they got off the bus. Every race day she'd go to a small, sealed, windowless room, more like a walk-in closet. The room contained a wooden table and chair, a stack of white envelopes, one hundred marked racing forms, and two-hundred-and-twenty-one-thousand dollars. When the shills got off the bus, they would line up in front of the room guarded by one of the beefy Chinese security guards. They would enter the room one at a time and receive an envelope of cash and the racing form marked with the day's bets.

Lucy's plan wasn't complicated. She'd short each enveloped the fifty bucks lunch money. When she counted out the funds, two-thousand-and-sixteen dollars went in an envelope, and fifty went inside her oversized bra or down her pants. This wasn't a South African diamond mine where everyone got a cavity search at the end of the day. Security was more concerned about the shills wandering around the track with Hong Mian money than with Lucy's ever-expanding chest.

She figured most of the shills didn't realize they were supposed to get the fifty bucks, and those that did were too scared to say anything about not getting it. After all, it wasn't like they were there by their own choice. Lucy thought the plan was clever in its simplicity. The shills had the money to place the bets and if they were stupid enough to keep some of the betting money, then they were the ones who'd get in trouble.

In addition to handing out the money Lucy was also responsible for collecting, counting, and placing the days receipts in a security bag along with the signed purchase agreements that turned the funds over to *The Thoroughbred Investment Corporation*.

AN OLD PLAYER IN A NEW GAME

8.
An Old Player In A New Game

Pluto's Deli on the corner of Spadina and College in the heart of Toronto's old garment district is Morris Rothman's go-to lunch spot. It advertised "The Biggest Muffins In The Solar System" a statement that by all accounts is most likely true. If the double rye corn beef sandwich with enough meat to delight even the greediest cardiologist didn't bring on chest pains, then the thousand calorie muffins that hardly fit on the plate would definitely have the middle-aged, overweight *schmatta* executives reaching for their nitroglycerin pills.

For all practical purposes, The Pluto, was Rothman's office. Of course he had an official place of business in a rented space across the street. The office was a small eight-by-ten room with a desk, chair, and computer, at the back end of a third-floor warehouse that specialized in selling promotional products and knock-off sports memorabilia made in China. The cardboard sign thumb tacked to the door read, Rothman Loan and Investment Company. But if you were looking for Morris, you went to The Pluto.

Every day Rothman would sit in the back of the nondescript deli holding court for financially strapped businessmen in need of his money-lending services, while at the same time, arranging high-stakes poker games for rich society lawyers and corporate executives that liked slumming with the colorful criminal element. The facts are these *gonifs* were as crooked and corrupt as the real criminals; they just did it with a contract rather than a Beretta. These Rosedale, Bridal Path, and Lawrence Park society types rarely lowered themselves to enter the ethnically pungent home of kishka, kasha varniskas and Montreal-style smoked meat.

Rothman runs the biggest gambling operation in Toronto, specializing in big money private poker parties for these wealthy degenerates, people that found The Pluto and the casino environment beneath their more cultured tastes. They usually just received a text message with a time and hotel room number for where the next big money event would take place. Men like Edward P. Tillerson III, scion of the late Edward Paul Tillerson who made his fortune the old fashion way, bootlegging, when Capone was king of Chicago and granddad was known as Short Pants Paulie because his six-foot-eight frame rarely found pants that came close to meeting his shoe tops.

The current Tillerson is the Director of the Woodbridge Downs Racing & Entertainment Complex. He and his Rosedale and Bridal Path friends preferred losing large sums of cash in a luxury suite in the King Charles Hotel surrounded by hot and hotter young ladies flown in from New York by Rothman's protector Albert The Artist Giacometti.

Giacometti is head of the New York Giacometti Crime Family that controlled the Montreal mob; but it also had interests in the open city of Toronto where the Sicilian Cosa Nostra and Calabrese Ndrangheta generally tolerated one another despite the longstanding vendetta between the Sicilian Fungo Family of Buffalo and the Calabrese Giacometti Family of New York.

On this particular day Giacometti was in Toronto to meet with Rothman to take in the evening's high stakes event at the King Charles. Rothman told Giacometti that the Woodbridge Track was having trouble competing with the revamped Crystal Beach operation and that Tillerson would be at the evening's festivities. When he heard his rival, Nicky Fungo and his Hong Mian friends were buying all the small racetracks in the province, he figured Tillerson might have need of his services.

The local Giacometti group ran the Canadian Pari-Mutuel Workers Union, a factor that might just create an opening for Giacometti to take control of Woodbridge on the pretext of helping Tillerson crush his competitor. Controlling horse racing and pari-mutuel wagering in Ontario would give the Giacometti Family a stranglehold on gambling throughout the North East.

Giacometti looked forward to lunch with Rothman at The Pluto. In the States once you left the five Burroughs it was almost impossible to get a genuine deli sandwich on real double rye. Once in Springfield Massachusetts on business, his people took him to a place that spread butter on the white bread that surrounded three small slices of meat that masqueraded as corn beef. He could have shot the waiter and as well as his subordinates.

Most people knew if Rothman is alone, he could be approached, but if he's with someone, it's prudent to stay clear. Leon Chao is neither prudent nor smart. He's no longer able to place bets with Kenny Kang so he figures he'll try Morris Rothman. He approaches Rothman's table and interrupts their coffee and muffin dessert. "Mr. Rothman I wonder if I could..."

Rothman finishes chewing a piece of his giant carrot muffin and without looking up speaks, "Fuck off! Can't you see we're eating?"

"But…"

Rothman looks at Chao with some curiosity, "You think I don't know who you are asshole, you're a deadbeat. Even if everyone on the street didn't know you owe the Chinese everything but your left testicle, I still wouldn't take your bet. You're a reprobate, do you even know what a reprobate is?"

Chao shakes his head. "No, but I have some information you might find of interest." Chao waits to be acknowledged.

"Get lost! You got nothing anybody wants to hear."

Chao turns to leave but Giacometti stops him. "Let's hear what the Chinaman's got to say. What's this big important news you want to tell us?"

Chao doesn't know who Giacometti is. "This is private, kind of a need to know thing."

Rothman almost chokes on his muffin. "Are you out of your fucking mind?"

Giacometti laughs and with one hand grabs a chair from the next table and places it in front of Chao. "Sit Chinaman!"

Chao looks at Rothman, not sure what to do.

Rothman looks at Giacometti, "Really… the guy's a punk."

Giacometti takes a paper napkin and wipes some muffin debris from the corner of his mouth. He looks at Chao and then at Rothman, "If it isn't important we'll take him out back, and demonstrate how they tenderize the meat in this joint."

Rothman points to the chair Giacometti supplied. "This better be fucking important."

Leon Chao sits and lay outs Yufu's plan for delivering shills to the racetrack. When he's finished Rothman peels off five hundred bucks from his stuffed money clip and tells Chao to be at The King Charles, Room 827, at eleven to discuss what else he knows about the Crystal Beach operation.

Giacometti looks at Rothman, "First time I ever got a Chinese fortune cookie in a Jewish deli."

CHAOS AT CRYSTAL

9.
Chaos At Crystal

Jesse's was nothing like her late father, the crooked rug entrepreneur Wally Nuts. Wally was a white trash opportunist with extreme social views and a peculiar asset management system that involved keeping a cache of gold Krugerrands, cash, and diamonds in an old Kelvinator buried under the floor in his bedroom. If Wally Nuts had any redeeming qualities, it was he was a shrewd businessman, and he loved his little girl, which is why he stashed the real money in a false wall in Jesse's bedroom.

Jesse was destined to a life on the other side of legal, but despite her colorful career path, she was by nature more generous, tolerant, and thoughtful than her miscreant Dad. Despite her more moderate temperament, mess with Jesse or her pals, and you might find a pearl-handled-switchblade playing tic-tac-toe with your vital organs.

When all was said and done, dear old Pop did teach Jesse one important lesson about running a business. His words repeated ad nauseam still echoed in her head, "People, Jesse… are the biggest problem in running a business, you got to get out of the office and on the floor. If you don't, they'll steal you blind, or bankrupt you with their incompetence. Business is not some collegial hippy commune, it's a bloody war… them against you."

Jesse understood all too well what her father meant, and if you worked for the Hong Mian, you can quadruple that sentiment in spades. Screw up and cost Benson Yeung a substantial payday, and you'd find yourself a pillar of the community, a cement pillar, even if you were a pretty blonde with Johnny Luck as your mentor.

As a consequence, Jesse did a daily walk-about with Zack Wei in tow, just to make an appearance and send the message that we're watching every fucking thing you do; so follow the rules, do what you're told, and you'll make it home without the need of an emergency room visit.

While on one of these walks, Jesse notices several of the Italians arguing with the Chinese. This wasn't good. When Jesse and Wei approach the disgruntled gathering, they quickly shut up.

"What's going on here?" asks Jesse.

The leader of the Chinese group responds, "Nothing Miss Jesse, everything is fine."

"Like hell!" complains one of the older Italian gentlemen. "Everything isn't fine. I have diabetes. I need my lunch."

Wei takes a menacing step toward the old man but Jesse puts her hand out to stop him from doing anything before she finds out the facts. "I don't understand your complaint. You each got fifty bucks to use for lunch or whatever you want. If you lost it betting that's on you."

"I didn't get any extra money. All I got was enough money for the bets."

By now a bunch of other shills joined the group wondering what was going on. One woman in the back pipes up, "I didn't even know we were supposed to get lunch money." Several others nod in agreement.

Jesse looks at Wei then back to the gathered crowd, "Did anybody here get lunch money?" Several people in the back muttered, "No not me…"

Jesse goes over to an ancient Chinese lady with a face like a dried walnut. "*Zunjing de zumu*, (Dear grandmother) did you get lunch money?"

The old lady smiles at Jesse's attempt to speak Chinese. She motions for Jesse to bend down to meet her barely four foot frame. She whispers in her ear, "*Méi qián* (No money) No my child, no money."

Jesse turns to Wei, "Take these people to the snack bar and get them something to eat. I'm going to find out what the hell is going on." The group of discontents is leery about following the hard looking Chinese lawyer but they're all hungry, so they follow. Jesse heads back to the office to find Milton and investigate what exactly is going on.

AN EVENING AT THE KING CHARLES

10.
An Evening At The King Charles

Rothman likes to keep is his poker games on the move. Rather than reserve one large luxury suite, he reserves three adjoining suites on lower floors so well-known clients can take the stairs avoiding any unwanted surveillance or awkward elevator rides. One room is reserved for poker, one for relaxing, and one for, shall we say, entertainment. The weekly game never takes place in the same rooms twice, and locations are shuffled between a half a dozen different luxury hotels. Just in case the Metro Police or RCMP got one of the hotel staff to squeal about the location, rooms are scanned for electronic listening devices a couple of hours before game time.

When players need a break, they can relax with the hostesses while consuming a Rye and Ginger Ale, or they can adjourn to the entertainment suite where they can enjoy the intimate company of the lady of their choice. You would think the women would be a big attraction but gamblers are generally focused on blowing their brains out at the table rather than being blown in the entertainment suite. The real purpose for the ladies is to pay attention. You never know what tidbits of information you can pick up from rich fools who drink too much, play lousy poker, and couldn't recognize a ringer if it was printed on his forehead.

Tonight there are a few extra people beyond the regular players. Rothman is there as always to supervise, Giacometti's girls are there, including one particular Chinese beauty Mai Ling, whose exotic charms are always in demand no matter how much money is lost. Leon Chao is there despite being completely out of his element, but the guest of honor is The Don, Albert The Artist Giacometti. All the players immediately recognize Giacometti from the newspaper pictures of him leaving the Manhattan courthouse after being found not guilty of the stabbing of state witness Vito Ratface Narducci.

Giacometti is a short, powerfully built, middle-aged man who wears ultra expensive Italian suites and custom shoes. He pays more to have his mop of thick silver hair cut every week than most people spend on their monthly mortgage. Rumor is when he was young, his barber cut his hair too short, making the up-and-coming mobster so angry he carved the man up so badly he went through the rest of his life looking like one of Picasso's Dora Maar portraits. There is no one brave enough to verify the veracity of the story, but true or not, from that time forward, Albert Giacometti was known as Albert The Artist Giacometti. Reputation is everything when it comes to maintaining power in the mob and Giacometti had the reputation.

As the men played poker, Rothman, Giacometti, and Chao discussed who the players were at the Crystal Beach Racetrack. The women bought drinks to the players, chatted with the ones taking a break, or excused themselves to the adjoining suite to help a big loser work out his frustrations.

Mai Ling made sure Giacometti, Rothman, and Chao's glasses were always full. Chao knew Yufu was behind the operation in Crystal Beach along with his Southern California associates, Benson Yeung and Johnny Luck. He didn't know anything about Nicky Fungo but he didn't have to, Rothman and Giacometti knew of the connection.

Chao told them about the pretty blonde ex-jockey that runs the place along with some old Jew accountant and a tough looking Chinese lawyer who is rumored to have been in a motorcycle gang when he was younger. He didn't know much about the broad, except she was pretty, a hard ass, and had the same name as some cowboy outlaw, Jesse something.

Giacometti and Rothman were familiar with most of the players. They figured they'd got as much as there was to get out of Chao for the time being. He was instructed to keep his eyes and ears open and report back with any details no matter how insignificant. When they finished their discussion Leon Chao took Mai Ling into the entertainment suite for a friendly nightcap.

The poker broke up at about eight o'clock in the morning. Some of the men went home while others went to work. Giacometti went back to his hotel room across town for a nap, and Rothman counted up the evening's take.

The girls called cabs that took them to the dock where they got on a ferry to the Billy Bishop Airport on Toronto Island. There, they waited in the lounge for a flight that would take them to Newark, NJ where they would take the long cab ride back into Manhattan.

While they waited for the flight to be announced, Mai Ling uses the lounge payphone to call Johnny Luck in California. Considering the time difference she sure as hell wasn't going to phone Benson Yeung or even his son Henry. The phone rings. It's answered.

"Johnny… it's Mai Ling in Toronto."

"You have something to report?"

"Rothman and Giacometti met with some Chinese guy, a Leon Chao. He looked like a nobody, but he seemed to have information, and both Giacometti and Rothman were very interested in what he had to say.

"Did you hear what they were talking about?"

"It sounded like this guy Chao had information on Crystal Beach, it was some kind of racetrack thing. I don't know if it's important, but I thought you and Mr. Yeung should know."

"Good girl Mai… they'll be a little extra bonus in your mailbox in a few days."

"I better go… the other girls are watching. I don't want them to get too curious."

"Understood. Things start going sideways, you get on a plane."

"Thanks Johnny, I'm glad the information is of interest."

They hang up. Mai Ling joins the other girls. One of the women who was watching Mai asks, "Who were you talking to?"

"Oh… I promised my mother I'd give her a call."

"She must be an early riser."

"She worries about me."

"I'd be very careful about making personal calls when you're on the clock if I was you."

"Yeah, you're right, but you know mothers."

MILTON SMELLS A RAT

11.
Milton Smells A Rat

Jesse is anxious to find out what is going on with the so-called missing lunch money. She knows Milton has been working on it for the last few days. She enters his office and flops down in one of the chairs across from Milton's desk piled high with computer reports and printouts. He removes his glasses and sighs.

"Jesse… I can't find anything that's missing. Sure some of the shills screwed up a few of the bets but that's to be expected. It looks like all the money that was supposed to be bet was bet. We did much better than we figured by the way so the boys will be happy."

Jesse isn't satisfied. "But what about this lunch money business? I don't like it. It makes us look sloppy."

Wei enters the office and takes the other seat across from Milton's desk.

"Anything?"

Milton shakes his head, "Nothing… *gornisht*!"

Jesse gets up and paces back and forth. "It's got to be the money hostess. She's got to be pocketing the lunch money. She must figure will never notice because all the bets are getting placed."

Wei scratches the back of his head. "I don't know Jesse, that seems like a big gamble for someone like her, she's not even a gambler, she's just a relative."

Milton sits back in his brown leather executive chair. "Desperate people do desperate things. But think about it. It's smart. She's in a closed room by herself. No one is watching except the guard and he's outside. She can do anything she wants, but she's a clever bitch. She doesn't grab a whole pile of cash and try to make a getaway, no sir, she steals small amounts from every shill and as far as we're concerned the bets are being placed and the money's being cleaned. If it wasn't for the brouhaha you guys ran into, we never would have known something was wrong."

Wei asks, "How much are we talking about?"

Milton puts on his glasses, grabs his calculator, and starts punching in numbers. "If she's taking all the lunch money, which is the smart thing to do. You don't want some people getting it and some not. Most people would chalk it up to us being cheap assholes. The players who were bitching never figured they'd run into you two."

"So Milton…" asks Jesse, "what's the bad news.

"She's lifting five grand a day, that's two-hundred thousand for the season. That's real money."

Jesse is pissed, "God damn it. Who is this bitch?"

Wei already knows, "Lucy Chao, she's that degenerate, Leon Chao's sister-in-law. They must be in it together."

"Maybe" says Jesse, "Why don't you have a conversation with Leon and I'll have a little talk with the sister-in-law.

Milton looks worried. "Do you think it's possible you guys were set-up? I mean maybe the shills saw you coming and figured they'd run some kind of scam and make a few bucks."

"I don't think so Milt, the sweet little old Chinese woman I spoke to was pretty convincing."

"Yeah, so I'm a sweet little old Zadie and look what I do for a living. Why don't we install a camera in the money room and see exactly what she's doing? Once we're sure, we can deal with the situation appropriately."

Wei stands up, "I'll get the camera installed with a feed to Jesse's office. Better late than never."

"Once we know for sure," says Jesse, "we got to handle it discreetly. Nothing can come back to us."

By the time the next race day comes around the hidden camera is in place. Wei had the technical staff install a feed into Jesse's office so she can view what happens on her computer. On race day, Jesse, Milton, and Wei gather around the computer waiting for the first shill to enter the money room.

An older Chinese man enters and stands waiting as Lucy Chao counts out the money. She sticks it in an envelope and hands it to the man along with the racing form. The man leaves. She checks off the man's name from a list and the next shill enters. The procedure continues without incident.

"Everything looks kosher," says Wei.

Jesse is agitated. "Something's wrong. The bitch has to be doing something we can't see."

"Just wait," says Milton, "let's see what she does when she's finished.

The whole procedure takes almost an hour to get through one hundred people. When the last person leaves Lucy still has a stack of bills on the table. As soon as the door closes behind the last shill Lucy starts stuffing the extra cash into her bra and down her pants.

Jesse jumps up from her desk, "I'll kill the bitch!"

Wei looks at her, "What happened to handling it discreetly?"

"Fuck that, she's a thief!"

Milton and Wei smile, "Jesse my dear," says Milton, "we're all thieves." Jesse never thought of herself as a thief just an honest criminal, but the truth of Milton's comment couldn't be denied. She calms down to a mere slow burn."

Wei speaks. "First, we have to find out if this Lucy Chen Chao broad is in partnership with her deadbeat brother-in-law or one of the other Chao relatives."

Milton looks at Wei like he just took a dump on the desk. "What did you say?"

Wei looks at him, "What?"

"What did you call her?"

"Lucy Chao."

"No you called her Lucy Chen Chao."

"So what, her maiden name is Chen. She's Lucy Chen Chao."

"Jesus Christ, we better get Yufu and Luck involved in this."

"What's the big deal?" asks Jesse and Wei almost simultaneously.

"You two wouldn't know or remember but a few years back Peter Pretty Boy Chen was murdered at the Green Dragon Restaurant with Benson Yeung sitting not more than fifteen feet away. The case is still open, and no one was ever arrested, but word was Peter Chen was involved with a bunch of people that wanted to steal the legendary ruby-filled Guan Yu. Lucy Chen is Peter Chen's sister. She disappeared after the murder."

"I thought that statute was just a legend."

Milton looks at Wei like he's crazy. "You want to be the one to ask Benson Yeung?"

"Hell no! I'm not stupid."

"Maybe it's just a coincidence," says Jesse.

"In our business, there's no such thing as coincidences," says Wei.

AJ REAPPEARS

12.
AJ Reappears

The YLYF partners have a lot riding on the Crystal Beach operation. If everything goes as planned, the small beach town could be turned into Las Vegas North, and why not? Vegas was a desert cow town and not much else; its only redeeming assets were gambling, girls, and proximity to Los Angeles. Crystal Beach has racing, casino gambling, girls, drugs, and proximity to Toronto, the Golden Horseshoe, and upstate New York. All the elements for creating a profitable money machine were in place. Never mind Vegas, Crystal Beach had the potential to be bigger than Lansky's old Havana operation.

It was already becoming the place for young professionals to party. The almost ubiquitous availability of the party drug ecstasy certainly helped to enhance its growing reputation as the good-time party town. At the moment it wasn't fancy or glitzy like Vegas, in fact it was a dump, but even that seemed to be an attraction. Colorful race track people and their associates gave the visitors the feeling of taking a weekend stroll on the wild side, with gambling, drugs, women, and the beach as the main attractions.

Located in the heart of the densely populated Golden Horseshoe, ninety minutes from Toronto, and ten minutes from the USA border, made Crystal Beach a prime investment opportunity for the YLYF group, both for their legal and extralegal operations. The town was on its way to becoming the next big playground for the rich and reckless. Property was cheap, especially compared to the sky-high real estate in Toronto and the almost as high prices of the northern cottage country. The ready availability of freshly laundered cash allowed YLYF to buy as much property as it wanted. With their resources the group could own the town and the politicians that run it.

Jesse didn't have much time to enjoy the beach or take in the local sites. She was just too busy learning her new job while putting out fires at the track, like the lunch money thief, an issue that still needed to be resolved.

Jesse lives in the gated Beach Yacht Club community. Being an ex jockey Jesse was used to getting up at the crack of dawn, she often arrived at the track before the sun came up. She had most of her meals in the Club House dining room where the staff catered to her every epicurean desire. By the time she got home late at night she was too mentally exhausted to do anything but watch television or sit on the back porch and watch Lake Erie roll onto the beach.

Now and then she had to get away from the track. Her favorite getaway was the restored Guardhouse Cookhouse, a stone and brick building dating back to the War of 1812. For an added touch of authenticity they re-purposed the old cells as private dinning areas. The place became popular amongst the jockey's who received deep discounts for their drinks as they contributed to the exotic atmosphere the weekend visitors craved.

It wasn't one of the usual earthy hangouts the jocks generally frequented, but it was the perfect place for a clandestine meeting for riders looking to do some business. Jesse liked the food, but deep down she knew the real reason she went to the Guardhouse was to keep an eye on outliers intent of cashing in on some long shots.

Jesse received a call earlier in the week from Johnny Luck in California. He told Jesse about Mai Ling's report and to be on the lookout for anything out of the ordinary. Under the circumstances Jesse felt she had to tell Johnny about Lucy Chen Chao. Things were happening quickly and they could go sideways fast.

Jesse sat off to the side by herself at a table for two. She enjoyed her Veal Marsala smothered in Shiitake mushrooms with a side of linguini and grilled peppers, washed down with a carafe of Pinot Noir. Across the restaurant a lively party was going on in the private dining area known as Cell Block 3. Jesse recognized the group was made-up of jockeys from the track. The host had his back turned to Jesse so she couldn't see his face, but his voice sounded very familiar. If he was, who she thought he was, she would not be happy. Jesse slips her waiter a twenty-dollar bill and asks him to checkout Cell Block 3.

The waiter arrives back at Jesse's table, "Miss James… They're all jockeys, most of them have been in here before, except for the fellow who's paying. He looks like a jockey too. They all call him AJ."

The hairs on the back of Jesse's neck stand straight up. She thanks the waiter and leaves a generous tip. Avellino Jose Gonzalez – AJ, is the son-of-a-bitch that ended her racing career by putting her through the fence at Hancock Downs. What the hell was he doing here? Jesse feels her heart pounding and her head throbbing.

He couldn't ride; he's suspended for five years; as far as Jesse is concerned, it should be for life. Johnny promised retribution at the right time, but Jesse couldn't just let this pass. Maybe he was acting as a jockey's agent and he was trolling for clients, or maybe he was trying to fix some races for some out-of-town interests. Maybe it had something to do with what Mai Ling told Johnny?

She had to do something quickly. She knew she should call Johnny and Yufu, but fuck that; this son-of-a-bitch tried to kill her. She pours the remaining Pinot Noir into a fresh glass the waiter left on the table. She slips the pearl handled switchblade out of her boot. She takes the linen napkin and drapes it over her arm while she palms the pearl handle. She picks up the fresh glass of Pinot Noir in her other hand and makes her way over to where all the jockeys are sitting. She opens the iron bars to the private dining room with the hand holding the switchblade. The jockeys sitting around the table all recognize her, and most of them are aware of the history between AJ and Jesse.

They all stop talking except AJ. "So boys... we all in for making some real dough?"

Jesse bends over placing the glass of Pinot Noir in front of AJ. "Complements of the house AJ." Her hand still palming the pearl handle comes around in front. She removes the linen napkin with her other hand while releasing the knife's six inch blade. Click.

The shiny razor sharp steel blade slips out of its hiding place. Jesse places it tight up against AJ's neck. She grabs the back of AJ's hair and pulls his head back as far as it can go. The blade is right up against his skin, so tight that in creates a small red sliver of dark blood. "Fucking move a muscle and I'll slit your goddamn throat. Don't move. Don't talk. Don't breathe."

A couple of the jockeys get up as if to come to AJ's rescue. "Sit the fuck down!" They obey.

"Gentlemen, if this poor man's mafia-style Appalachian summit is intended to organize a race fixing scheme? I would seriously reconsider."

She turns her attention back to AJ. The knife up against AJ's neck cuts just a little deeper. "You're breathing asshole, I told you not to breathe."

The waiter arrives. He looks at Jesse with the knife up against AJ's throat. "I guess you gentlemen are just about finished. I'll get the check." He leaves.

"Gentlemen, let's have a roll call, one at a time around the table. I'd like you to acknowledgement you understand the situation. Say 'Yes Jesse, I understand.' So let's start with you as she looks at one of the men." One at a time the men acknowledge their understanding.

"Gentlemen, you can all leave, but if I, or my people, ever see you talking to Mr. Gonzalez again, you will be very sorry you did." The men all get up and leave.

Jesse turns her attention back to AJ. "I want to know who you're working for?" The knife is so tight to AJ's neck that it's difficult for him to talk."

"Rothman and Giacometti," he squeaks, 'it's Rothman and Giacometti."

Jesse doesn't quite get it. "Giacometti wants to fix races here… that doesn't make sense. Why?"

"I don't know. Rothman's a gambler, he wants to make money."

"What about Giacometti? What does he want?"

"I guess he wants the same thing – make money."

"That's all?"

"I guess… but he said something else about disrupting your plans and taking over the track."

"You're done here, understand? Pack you bags and get the hell out of the country tonight and don't come back. Don't contact Rothman, Giacometti, or anyone else associated with them. Nod if you understand." AJ nods.

Jesse continues. "You fucked with the wrong girl my friend. You're a dead man walking. You can keep looking over your shoulder for however long you've got left on this earth, but it won't help. You wouldn't see it coming. Bang! And you're dead. It's as simple as that. So pack your bags and disappear." Jesse removes the knife from AJ's neck, retracts the blade, and slips it in her pocket.

UNION TROUBLE

13.
Union Trouble

AJ is in trouble. It's a question of who's the biggest threat: Jesse in Crystal Beach, Benson Yeung and Johnny Luck in Los Angeles, or Giacometti and Rothman in Toronto. In the end AJ figures he's better off sticking with Giacometti and Rothman as he still could be of some use to them. He calls Rothman who tells him to be at the *Il Nostro Salotto* at ten-thirty.

The *Il Nostro Salotto* is a downtown mob hangout owned by one of Giacometti's Toronto lieutenants. The place is just about what you'd expect: dark and expensive. The walls are sandblasted brick covered in what looks like Leroy Neiman images of picturesque Calabria. The banquets and matching chairs are tufted maroon leather and the waiters are decked out in black slacks and shirts open at the neck. Gino, the manager, figured adding a white silk tie to the waiters' outfits would be just a little theatrical even though most of the clientele acted and dressed like they were in a Scorsese film.

The coat-check girl looked like she just stepped out of a Bogie movie with her short black skirt and matching silk shirt straining to keep her assets in place. If smoking weren't banned in all such eating establishments, you just knew there'd be a sexy cigarette girl walking around hawking her wares.

AJ sits alone nervously waiting like a man on death row after finishing his final meal. Rothman and Giacometti enter the restaurant and are greeted like the Pope and his senior Cardinal. The staff does everything but kiss Giacometti's four-carat diamond ring. The two men join AJ at the table set aside for senior Mafioso meetings.

A man in his late forties and a woman in her mid twenties enter the restaurant and head straight for the bar. The woman takes a seat with her back to Giacometti's table while her companion sits opposite with a direct view of the gangster, gambler, and jockey.

On the surface they look like an ordinary upper middle-class Chinese couple having a few drinks after a night at the theatre, but if you remove the expensive clothes, you would find both the man and the woman are covered in Chinese Foo Dog tattoos, a sign both are members of Zack Wei's old Lion Dog Motorcycle Club. They order a couple of Stoli Screwdrivers. The man takes out his cell phone equipped with the EarSpy audio distance monitoring application. He plugs in a single ear bud and places the phone on the bar with the microphone aimed in Giacometti's direction. He fiddles with a few of the controls filtering out the ambient restaurant noise. For anyone who's watching, he's just another self-absorbed putz ignoring his attractive companion while he listens to music.

Rothman and Giacometti order Rye and Gingers. Giacometti strokes his chin as he sizes up the jockey. "You fucked up!"

"I did exactly what you told me to do. I met with the jocks and arranged for the first round of fixes. How the hell was I supposed to know that bitch would be there? She never goes anywhere but the track and Yacht Club where she lives."

Rothman joins in. "She's a girl for Christ sake. Can't you handle some silly bitch without an armed escort?"

AJ opens his collar so they can see the still red scab on his neck where Jesse placed her blade. "She had knife to my throat!"

Giacometti laughs, "What, that little scratch? Jesus, I thought you jockeys were supposed to be tough." Giacometti takes a sip of his drink and motions to Rothman. "Guess we should have hired the broad instead of this pansy." Rothman nods in agreement.

"Make all the jokes you want, but this bitch is as tough as they come. She's not afraid of anything or anybody. She's got Johnny Luck and Stanley Yufu behind her. She's untouchable."

Giacometti considers AJ's defense. "No one's untouchable, not even Johnny Luck or that ancient Chinese antique, Benson Yeung. No one, understand, no one... we can get to anybody."

"Maybe so," says AJ, "but so can those Chinese bastards."

The guy at the bar smiles as he listens to the conversation. He thinks to himself, Wei will get a kick out of these goombahs flapping their gums like they knew what they were dealing with.

Giacometti drains the rest of his drink and waves it in the air signaling their waiter bring him a refill. Without removing his gaze from AJ, Giacometti asks Rothman, "So what do you want to do with this *stronzo*?"

"I don't know. He's not much use to us anymore. Maybe we just get rid of him."

"You think?" Giacometti considers the options. "He might be useful once we take over that beach operation. He knows the racing game." Giacometti sits back in his chair. He's made his decision. "Go back to LA and find something to do. We'll call you when we need you. Now get lost." AJ gets up and leaves. The couple at the bar order another round of drinks.

Ten minutes later the restaurant door opens and union boss Fat Tony Verde and his second-in-command Frankie Russo enter the restaurant. Fat Tony is President of the Canadian Pari-Mutuel Workers Union. The two men go directly to the back of the restaurant where Rothman and Giacometti are sitting. There are boisterous greetings, and the usual double-cheek kisses. The men order sixteen-ounce steaks and two bottles of Tignanello, 2005. Dessert is huge slices of Black Forest cake and coffee. Over brandy and cigars they discuss the strike and shutdown of the Crystal Beach racetrack. No one says anything about the cigars. The couple at the bar continues to monitor the meeting.

CHANGING OF THE GUARD

14.
Changing Of The Guard

The mob-union parley finally breaks up at about twelve-forty-five. Giacometti and Rothman are picked-up by a driver in a black Lincoln Continental. Fat Tony is too fat to make it back to his car without the aid of a mobile defibrillator so he waits to be picked up by Frankie Russo in front of the *Il Nostro Salotto*.

The Chinese couple follows the two union executives out of the restaurant. The woman opens her purse and takes out a cigarette. She asks Fat Tony if he has a light. He doesn't notice her companion repositioning himself on the other side and slightly behind him. Tony lights the woman's cigarette. She takes a puff, blows out some smoke, and searches in her purse for her Beretta 92FS. She finds the weapon, removes it from her purse and jabs it into the mound of blubber that overflows Fat Tony's too-tight suit pants.

Fat Tony Verde looks down at the Beretta penetrating his expanse of *schmaltz*. "What the fuck is this?"

The woman's companion rams his matching firearm into Fat Tony's other side. "Shut-up and listen. Your plan to shut down Crystal Beach is not going to happen."

"How the hell do you know about that?"

"That's our business. You just do what we tell you to do."

"You're crazy. I'm not going against Albert Giacometti and Rothman. I don't do what I'm told, they'll kill me and get someone else to do it."

The Chinese triggerman thinks for a minute. "Yah… that could happen."

Frankie Russo pulls up in a silver Cadillac Escalade. The male gunsel gets in the front and points his Beretta at Russo. The woman orders Fat Tony to cram his fat ass into the backseat. He resists but she nudges him with the muzzle of her automatic.

Her partner orders Russo to drive to an abandoned waterfront brick factory that's sat empty for years. They drive in silence for five minutes.

Fat Tony sizes up the woman. She's slightly built and no match for his bulk. Gun, or no gun, she'd be easy to overpower. He could take the gun away and put a bullet in the back of her partner's head. He had to do something. Send a message to these Chinese punks and show them how real gangsters play the game.

What Fat Tony didn't realize was the attractive young woman was no virgin when it came to dealing with fat slobs who thought their size and inflated egos were too much for her to handle. The Beretta and the hidden brass knuckles she managed to slip on to her other hand were all she needed. Tony makes his move.

"Listen… you're an attractive broad. You know what my people do to dames like you. You stick your pretty Oriental nose in where it doesn't belong and you'll hope they just kill you." Tony grabs for the gun but the woman is expecting the move. The hand with the brass knuckles whips across her body landing directly under Fat Tony's nose. There's a momentary gasp from the fat man, then nothing. Silence. Blood pours out of his nose.

Her partner turns to see what happened. As he does, Fat Tony springs to life like a man possessed. He grabs the woman by the throat in an attempt to choke the life out of her. Her associate puts his gun to Frankie Russo's head, "You just drive."

Fat Tony is on top of the woman in the backseat of the Caddie banging her head against the soft leather seat. Blood, snot, and disgusting sludge drips out of Fat Tony's nose all over the woman's dress. She unloads her Beretta into Fat Tony's chest. Bang! Bang! Bang! His bulk goes limp on top of her. With some effort she pushes him onto the floor of Caddie.

"The son-of-a-bitch ruined my dress."

Her partner looks at her and then at the corpse of Fat Tony Verde. "Yah, I liked that dress."

They arrive at the brickworks. The male gunman tells Frankie Russo to pull over in front of the derelict building. He looks at his female colleague. "You better call it in."

The woman retrieves her phone from her purse and dials. The phone rings. "It's me... a little... not any more... let's just say Elvis has left the building... no the banjo player is still with us. Okay, I'll tell him."

Thirty-six hours later, three teenage boys investigating the remains of the derelict building find Fat Tony's bullet riddled body lying on the floor of the abandon Waterfront Brickworks.

At just about the same time Frankie Russo, the acting head of the Canadian Pari-Mutuel Workers Union, local 137, holds a press conference announcing a wildcat strike of all the cashiers and ticket window agents at the Woodbridge Downs Racing & Entertainment Complex, thereby effectively shutting down the racetrack and the adjacent casino whose workers will not cross the picket line. Rothman and Giacometti are not happy, and neither is Edward P. Tillerson III, Chairman of the Board of the Woodbridge Downs Racing & Entertainment Complex.

THE HIT LIST

15.
The Hit List

There are two kinds of mob organizations, old school gangs like the Hong Mian, that that prefer sophisticated schemes that involve clever planning and implementation, saving the rough-stuff for a last resort; and new school operations like the Giacometti Crime Family that cut right to the chase by intimidating, threatening, and murdering as a standard first move maneuver; just so you understand they're serious. But make no mistake, old school or new, you threaten to take over a rival's territory and that challenge will be greeted with blood-spattered retribution.

In the case of Giacometti's attempt to take control of Crystal Beach, the response was swift and effective, resulting in one dead union boss and an unforeseen disquieting turn of events: Woodbridge was now under siege. Strikers marched with signs declaring their ill treatment at the hands of bootlegger offspring Edward P Tillerson III. Poor Eddie Tillerson's wife could hardly show her face at the weekly Mahjongg get-together with the girls; the 'poor-dear' insincerities of her society friends almost drowned out the clicking of small ivory tiles. Of course the loss of millions of dollars for the racetrack, government, and their backroom underworld operators was more than embarrassing, it was costly, both financially and reputationally.

A decision had to be made. The attempt to take over Crystal Beach failed. Are Giacometti and Rothman willing to go to war in order to remain in control of Woodbridge; or are they willing to negotiate a peace accord in order to maintained the Status quo?

Giacometti, the artist, whose palette consisted of one color, blood red, wanted to strike hard and fast; while Rothman, the odds player, cautioned restraint with a cost-benefit approach. Crystal Beach aside, the Woodbridge challenge had to be answered in blood. Going to war meant going up against the entire international Hong Mian operation, plus Buffalo's Fungo Crime Family.

The consequences of failure could be disastrous. In the end, war or peace, someone on the other side had to die, if for no other reason than to save face. Allowing YLYF to take over or even disrupt Woodbridge sent a message to other rival organizations that the Giacometti Family was weak and vulnerable to attack. It didn't matter who started the brawl, it only mattered who was left standing when it was over.

Giacometti calls a war council to decide who was going to pay the ultimate price. The murder of Fat Tony Verde had to be answered even if the ultimate objective was a return to the prewar tenuous co-existence. Who should they hit: Frankie Russo, the union turncoat; Stanley Yufu, Canadian Hong Mian Operations Manager, triad status Vanguard; Zack Wei, lawyer and Chief Hong Mian Enforcer, triad status the Red Pole; Nicky The Mushroom Fungo, Underboss of the Buffalo Fungo Crime Family; or should it be Jesse James, the ex jockey and current Director of the Crystal Beach Racetrack, triad status Blue Lantern?

In addition to Giacometti and Rothman, Eduardo Four-Fingers Segreti, Giacometti's Underboss; Mickey Caplan, Rothman's partner, accountant, and fence; and Edward P. Tillerson III, Director of the Woodbridge Downs Racing & Entertainment Complex are at the meeting. It's quickly decided that despite his Benedict Arnold act, Frankie Russo would be left untouched, at least until the current strike and its media focus devolved into back-page news. Ultimately Eddie Russo would turn-up facedown in the Don River, with a revolver in his hand and a gapping whole in his head.

"I say cut off the Dragon's head," pronounces Giacometti, "we hit Benson Yeung in LA and Stanly Yufu here in Toronto. Without their leadership the whole organization will fall apart." Giacometti can afford to be cavalier about murdering the top echelon Hong Mian leaders in Los Angeles and Toronto. When things finally settle down, Albert The Artist Giacometti will be safely tucked away in his cozy, ten-acre fortress estate on Long Island, or in his Scilla Cliffside Villa enjoying the alternate, and sometime simultaneous, pleasures of his two French mistresses. In either case, he'll be almost completely insulated from just about anything but an aerial attack.

"Easy for you to say Albert, you'll be in Southern Italy banging the *fanculo*-sisters. The rest of us have to take the heat back here. Besides killing Benson Yeung and Yufu still leaves Benson's son Henry, who'd be out for blood, and Johnny Luck who runs all day-to-day operations. If we have to take somebody out, it's got to be somebody on the level of Fat Tony."

Caplan adds his two cents, "What about the lawyer, Zack Wei?"

"Possible," says Rothman, "but then we'll have all those nuts from the Lion Dogs motorcycle gang after us, in addition to the Hong Mian. You really want every poker game we run raided by those crazy Chinese bastards."

Giacometti jumps back in, "We can't touch any of the Fungo crew, that's too close to home. I'd have the Commission on my ass."

"So who the hell does that leave?" Asks Caplan.

"Segreti finally speaks up, "What about the broad?"

Silence. Each man mulls over the idea of killing Jesse James. She's high enough up the food chain to make an impact and send a message, but not high enough to go to war for. She's just a dame, and she's not even Chinese or Italian. Yeung and Fungo will just chalk it up to collateral damage and move on to business as usual, at least, that's what the wise men of the Rothman-Giacometti alliance figured, but did they figure correctly?

THE SOKOLOVS

16.
The Sokolovs

The El Al flight from Tel Aviv to Toronto was long. It would have been more comfortable in business class but Sasha was always trying to save money. Simcha kept telling her not to worry, they'd always have clients: somebody always needed killing. For some reason Toronto gambler Morris Rothman and his Calabrese cronies wanted some ex female jockey killed. The Sokolovs didn't care why, that wasn't their business, but Simcha was hesitant. He didn't like killing women, but Sasha insisted, the money was good, and that was all she really needed to know – women, men, it didn't matter. She drew the line on kids; people who wanted to murder children were monsters. She was just a businesswoman; it just happened her business was contract murder.

Sasha and Simcha Sokolov were the best when it came to killing. They always worked as a pair, and they always got the job done. Word was they were twins or maybe husband and wife; they were also rumored to be Russian with ties to the Bratva, or as some have speculated ex Mossad operatives that started their own entrepreneurial enterprise. Nobody really knew anything about the pair. All you really needed to know was, they got the job done.

If you were a client, you'd receive an advertisement for drain cleaner every week containing a series of numbers that related to a line on a page in the book, The Beastly Beatitudes of Balthazar B, by J.P. Donleavy. At the bottom of the page was a 1-800 phone number that changed every week. If you needed the services of the Sokolovs you phoned that number and left a message quoting the required line in the book along with the name and location of the person or persons that were to be eliminated. If the reply seemed legit, you'd receive a new text message with a price that was to be paid to a predetermined Cayman Island bank account.

There was never any other contact or conversation; everything was done by text. There were no pictures, no permanent addresses, no permanent phone numbers - no permanent anything. The Sokolovs changed their look, clothes, hairstyles, and cover names like most people change their underwear. In short they were ghosts.

Nobody even knew if Sokolov was their real name, but that was the name you needed to know if you wanted to do business. For this particular job, their passports read Dr. and Mrs. Nigel Carson. You could use local talent to knock somebody off, but it was dangerous. It was better, if possible, to bring someone in from out of town and the Sokolovs were as far out of town as you could get. They were expensive, but they were worth it. They'd fly in, do the job, and fly out – bing, bang, boom, with the emphasis on the bang and the boom.

They arrived in Toronto, rented a car, and drove to a UPS store with rent-by-the-month mailboxes where they picked up a package left for them by Rothman. The parcel contained two Smith and Wesson semi-automatics and two shoulder holsters, a photograph of Jesse and her black Audi TT, and a list of places she frequented, including the Guardhouse Cookhouse. Fully equipped with their requested tools of the trade, they got on the 401, went south to towards the lake on the 400 to the Queen E and headed for Crystal Beach.

By the time they got to Crystal Beach it was late and the last race of the evening had been run. They figured Jesse would either go home or head for a place like the Guardhouse. They spotted Jesse's sports car in front of the Guardhouse. They parked and casually walked over to the Audi checking to make sure it was her car.

Zack Wei and his wife, Ginger, finished eating dinner and were walking to their car when Wei notices the handsome couple checking out Jesse's car. Instead of driving home immediately, he sits and waits.

Wei's wife understood her husband was in a dangerous business. "What's wrong?"

"That couple checking out Jesse's car, I don't like it."

"It's a nice car Zack, people like to look at cars like that."

"Sure they do, but I still don't like it." Wei takes out his phone and dials Milton Goldstein's phone number. "Hi Milt, it's me, Zack. I'm in the Guardhouse parking lot, Jesse's in trouble, can you come pick up my wife and take her home? No, I won't need any help, just the lift for Ginger." He looks at his wife. She's worried but doesn't say a word. "Thanks Milt, hurry."

Wei texts Jesse, 'Danger... good looking couple, well dressed, checking out your car. Smells off, I've got your back – Zack.'

Inside the Guardhouse Jesse sits at the bar enjoying a Vodka Collins and some peanuts. Her phone vibrates, She see's Zack's text. She doesn't turn around or make any sudden moves. She continues sipping her drink and occasionally says hello to some of the staff that know who she is. Johnny called her earlier in the week from LA to warn her to be careful, Giacometti was a hothead and he was bound to try something. She told him not to worry, Zack and Yufu warned her already.

The well-dressed couple enters the restaurant, look around, and head to the bar. The woman: attractive with black hair and just the right amount of makeup, wearing black slacks, black shirt, and black leather bomber jacket takes the seat beside Jesse. Her companion: a handsome mid forties man wearing black slacks, white shirt, and grey sport's jacket takes the seat beside the woman. The two looked remarkably similar, almost like they were twins.

The woman touches Jesse's arm, "Excuse me Miss, but I understand a lot of people from the track hangout here. Is that true?"

Jesse turns just in time to get a quick glimpse of the leather strap indicating the woman is wearing a shoulder holster.

"That's right, quite a few come here."

The woman's male companion joins into the conversation "How about you, do you work at the track?"

"As a matter of fact I do?"

"I apologize, we're being very impolite, not to mention nosey. I'm Nancy Carson and the handsome devil at my side is my husband Nigel." They all shake hands and make the usual small talk pleasantries. They offer to buy Jesse a drink but she declines on the pretext of driving home. They buy her one anyway.

The conversation is pretty mundane, just a couple of tourists that heard about Crystal Beach and the racetrack, and figured they'd check it out before heading off for a romantic weekend in Niagara Falls. Jesse goes along with the charade. Jesse knows Zack is outside waiting so she figures it's time to put and end to whatever is going on.

"Well it was nice meeting you but I have to get up at the crack of dawn so I'll say goodnight."

The woman grabs Jesse's arm a little harder than she intended. Jesse gives her a look. "Sorry... don't know my own strength but we'd love to see shed row and the horses, think you could sneak us in?" The woman still has a hold of Jesse's arm.

"Sorry... that's impossible." Jesse starts to move away but the woman's grip tightens and her partner moves to block her way. The man brushes back the front of his sport's jacket revealing the S&W semi automatic dangling from his shoulder holster. The woman does the same. The man smiles, "I'm sure it's possible, Jesse. Let's go for a ride."

The bartender notices something is off. "Everything okay Jesse?"

"Sure Hank. Everything is fine."

The man drops more than enough cash on the bar to cover the drinks. With one Sokolov on either side Jesse is escorted out of the Guardhouse Cookhouse.

As they leave the restaurant, Jesse sees Zack's Cadillac waiting with the engine running. Jesse is pushed into the back seat of the rented Chevy Malibu, Sasha Sokolov pushes in beside her with her S&W semi automatic aimed at Jesse's chest. Simcha takes the driver's seat and they head for the track. Zack follows from a discreet distance. Zack taps the hands free phone connection on his steering wheel. "It's me. It looks like they're going to the track. Head them off at Rebelstock and Ridgeway."

The Malibu stops at the corner of Ridgeway and Rebelstock. Parked at the Crystal Palace Ice Cream Parlor on the corner of the intersection is a group of nine leather clad Chinese Lion Dog Motorcycle Club members lead by Genghis The Khan Lee. As the Malibu makes a right onto to Rebstock, Lee signals his fellow club members to follow. Zack Wei's Cadillac takes a position behind the bikers. The Sokolovs can't help but notice.

Jesse speaks up, "I see you noticed my friends. I suggest you pull over so we discuss options." Lee and two of his associates pull up beside the Malibu only inches away from the car. The rest of the motorcycles are right on the Malibu's tail with Wei's Caddie close behind.

Sasha is distracted by the bikers and doesn't notice Jesse casually reaching into her boot for the pearl handled switchblade, "Don't be stupid, you can still get out of this alive." Simcha guns the engine in an attempt to outrun the motorcycles.

Sash turns angrily jamming the gun up under Jesse's chin, "Shut the fuck up!" But Jesse responds quickly. Click. Before Sasha realizes what's happening Jesse slashes Sasha's wrist. She drops the gun. Blood spurts all over Sasha, Jesse, and the backseat of the Malibu. Sasha grabs her wrist with her other hand trying to stop the bleeding. Jesse grabs Sasha's black hair ramming her head backwards into the headrest as her knife hand comes across slamming into Sasha's nose. Sasha goes limp.

Simcha is busy navigating the unlit country road trying to force the bikers into a ditch but without success. He turns to see what's going on in the backseat just in time to see Jesse's knife hand heading towards his face. Everything goes black.

The next thing Jesse remembers is Zack Wei pulling her out of the Malibu that's lying almost perpendicular in a ditch at the side of the darken country road. Simcha Sokolov is bloodied and groggy from a head contusion from the crash. His hands are bound behind his back and three of the bikers are standing guard. Another biker is on the phone calling for a Lion Dog tow truck to come and recover the Malibu while two other Lion Dogs are working on Sasha to slow the bleeding from her wrist.

Jesse is bruised and her head is throbbing. There is blood dripping from her nose but she is substantially free of serious injury. Wei has already called a local track veterinarian to come and get the woman. Within five minutes the vet and three cars with several more Lion Dog Club members arrive. The vet and two bikers take the woman and drive off. The man is put into the trunk of one of the other cars and that car leaves escorted by the remaining bikers. Wei helps Jesse into his car and he drives her home.

NEW RECRUITS

17.
New Recruits

The basement of the Guardhouse Cookhouse is a dreary subterranean dungeon; a cold, damp place where the ghosts of captured enemy combatants from the War of 1812 still linger in the dank heavy air. The three-foot thick stonewalls somehow failed to keep out the creepy crawlers that called the place their home. It was the perfect place for an interrogation, beating, or execution.

The Dauphin family has run the restaurant for seventy-five years; unfortunately Max Dauphin's recent bad luck at the track created a cash shortfall that even the profitable eatery could not overcome. Max and his three daughters still ran the place and the Dauphin name was still on the title, but that was merely a formality. The real owner of the Guardhouse Cookhouse is YLYF Entertainment Corporation making it the ideal location for the kind of get-together that was about to take place.

Sitting in the middle of the room on empty wooden barrels with their hands tied behind their backs are Sasha and Simcha Sokolov, or if you prefer, Dr. and Mrs. Nigel Carson. Also present are Jesse James, Zack Wei, Genghis The Khan Lee, leader of the Lion Dogs Motorcycle Club, and Stanley Yufu.

Yufu, rubs his Jack Palance chin while sizing up the two assassins. "So you're the famous Sokolovs?" Sasha and Simcha don't answer. "Looks like you really screwed the pooch on this one." They still don't respond. Yufu turns to Jesse. "You're the one they tried to kill; do you want to do the honors?"

Jesse considers the idea. She is a hard-ass, but is she's a killer? It's one thing to threaten or to take someone out in self defense but she had no intention of killing two people with hands tied behind their backs. The others in the room had no such reservations. "They're just hired muscle. I want the son-of-a-bitch that gave the order."

Yufu thinks for a minute before responding. "Normally I'd tell Mr. Wei to look after this mess, and he would tell Mr. Lee to resolve the matter with a couple of bullets to back of your heads, but perhaps you could earn a reprieve by performing a few tasks in order that we may return to business as usual without any interference from your former employer. I need your answer now or I turn things over to my associates."

Simcha looks at Sasha who nods agreement. "We're in, who do you want eliminated?" Yufu doesn't answer. He turns to Wei. "Make the arrangements. Set them up at the Yacht Club but put a couple of Genghis's men on them till we know we can trust them. Either one steps out of line, kill'em both."

LUCY IS A LOSER

18.
Lucy Is A Loser

Despite the seemingly endless chaos that surrounds Jesse, she is still responsible for seeing everything at the Crystal Beach Race Track runs smoothly. There are of course problems beyond the normal day-to-day snafus that plague any organization that involves a lot of sketchy people. Jesse isn't sure who's worse, the customers or the employees. Managing the Crystal Beach track is like watching a bunch of three-year-olds run around waving a sharp scissors in the air. It's only a matter of time until something bad happens.

Luckily, Jesse had Milton Goldstein to keep an eye on things when she is otherwise consumed with Hong Mian business. The money laundering operation is proceeding as planned except for the Lucy Chao problem; and the ecstasy logistic system they installed is working well except for the Randy Lydia debacle.

One of Yufu's fillies, Randy Lydia died in Upstate
New York before the vets could remove the
shipment of ecstasy. The sack containing the
drugs broke, releasing the contents into the
animal's system causing a huge temperature
spike and ultimately a heart attack. At least the
animal managed to get through customs before it
died. Fungo's people managed to cover up the
mess before it got out of hand. They'd have to be
more careful about overloading the mules. But a
decision still had to made about Lucy Chen Chao.
Jesse's cell phone vibrates. She answers. "Hello…"

"Jesse, it's me." The voice on the line is Johnny
Luck.

"Boy, am I glad to hear your voice. It's a real
cluster fuck up here."

"Well, you may not be so happy to hear from me."

"Why? What's wrong?"

"AJ appealed his suspension, and he's been given
permission to ride… at least until the appeal is
heard next month."

"Son-of-a-bitch! Where's he riding? Maybe I'll
pay him a social call."

"No you won't! I told you he'd be dealt with and
he will. We just have to figure out an appropriate
retirement party."

There's an awkward pause. Jesse speaks, "You heard about Randy Lydia?"

"Sure I heard… it's no big deal. Sometimes these things happen. It's the cost of doing business. Just make sure the parcels meet the weight requirements."

There's another pause, "Where's AJ riding?"

"Florida, why?"

"I think I have a solution to the AJ situation."

"I have to meet with Nicky Fungo in Buffalo this week, how about we meet Thursday at the Rose Garden Chinese Eatery? I'll buy you dinner and we can discuss your idea in person." Jesse and Luck say goodbye and hang up.

The wheels for Jesse's revenge are set in motion, but she still had to deal with Lucy Chen Chao; the bitch is her responsibility, and it's important to prove to the men that she has the *cajones*, or as they say in Chinese, the *poli*, to do what's required.

She was still ticked-off about the Sokolovs. They tried to kill her. For all she knew, they still secretly planned to carry out the assignment they were paid to do. She should have taken Yufu up on his offer to eliminate the Russians, but she wasn't ready, she wasn't prepared to take that step. It was a mistake. It showed weakness. It made her look soft, and that was dangerous.

She could rationalize to herself that Sasha and Simcha Sokolov had skills that could be used. It was helpful that they had no connection to the Hong Mian. They were useful, Lucy Chao wasn't, but still, her refusal to accept Yufu's offer made her look weak. She had her chance, and she declined. These men all liked her, that she knew, but still, business came first, and weakness caused distrust. Johnny wasn't around to protect her. She had to cleanup her own mess. She had to prove to the men she really was one of them, and not just Johnny Luck's pet project. If she wanted to continue her rise up the Hong Mian latter Lucy Chen Chao must die.

Milton did the due diligence confirming Lucy Chao was in fact Lucy Chen, sister of the late Peter Pretty Boy Chen, the low level Hong Mian driver that got involved with a group of Maltese Falcon wannabes looking to steal the legendary, and perhaps mythical, Guan Yu statue filled with priceless Pigeon Blood rubies.

Lucy was Peter's sister, and it was understandable she'd hate the people who killed her brother, but her brother was a thief and worse, a turncoat, and that was something no criminal organization could or would tolerate. Jesse wasn't shy about using her pearl handled switchblade, but that was usually to defend herself, or like the Ellie Lang situation in LA to intimidate; but murder was different. Johnny warned her the time would come when she'd have to make the call herself, and that time had arrived. She picked up the phone and dialed Zack Wei's number.

"Zack, it's Jesse. Give your friend Genghis a call, someone has to take out the trash."

The following race day, Lucy Chen Chao did her usual one-for-you-and-one-for-me routine in the money shed, but instead of the usual track security personnel, the shed was manned by two of Genghis Lee's Lion Dog club members dressed in track security uniforms. As Lucy left the makeshift shed with hundred dollar bills stuffed into her bra and panties, the two motorcycle thugs took her by the arms and whisked her off, never to be seen, or heard from again.

When her husband, Arthur, arrived home there was a note on the bed written in a Chinese script that he knew was not his wife's. Loosely translated the note said she was leaving him for another man. Later that day her brother-in-law, Leon Chao, was found face down in the mud under the Rosedale Valley Bridge.

A BAD HAND AT THE KING CHARLES

19.
A Bad Hand At the King Charles

It's poker night at the King Charles and the usual suspects are all in place. Morris Rothman, Edward P. Tillerson III, and the Giacometti girls, including the lovely Mai Ling are all present. Tillerson is nervous, he excuses himself from the game and approaches Rothman who's sitting enjoying a Rye and Ginger while chatting up one of the ladies. Nobody notices Mai Ling casually unlocking the door to the suite. Tillerson takes the seat beside Rothman.

"Where's Albert?"

Rothman takes a sip of his drink, "He took off for Italy this morning."

"Does he expect trouble?"

"He always expects trouble."

"I understand a certain ex female jockey stills walks among us."

"These things take time."

"You don't think they just fucked off with the money, do you?"

Rothman laughs, "You think they'd cross Giacometti? Nobody is that stupid. Be patient?"

The door bursts open and four men enter, each holding an automatic weapon. Two of the men are dressed as Metro Police Officers while the other two are in plain clothes. If you looked real close, the uniforms didn't quite look right, and the usually clean-cut plain-clothes officers displayed a certain rough scruffiness that made them look more like motorcycle gang bangers, which is exactly what they are. The fact that all four men are Chinese is probably a dead give-away as to their identity as Lion Dog Club members. The ruse is hopefully good enough to get them in and out of the hotel without anyone interfering.

One of the men in a suit takes the lead, "This is a raid! Everybody facedown on the floor with your hands on your heads!" The women aren't strangers to police raids so they nonchalantly comply. The men more scared their wives will find out than they are off the police also meekly obey.

One of the men dressed as a cop collects the people in the lounge room while the other pseudo cop interrupts a couple in the bedroom. One of the uniformed cops confiscates everyone's phone including any Apple Watches, just in case some smart-ass thought he could use it to call for help. The other cop rips the hotel phone out of the wall. Everyone is on the floor as instructed except for Tillerson who starts to complain. "Do you know who I am? If you don't leave these people alone, I'll call your Chief and you can kiss your pension good bye."

The leader of the group approaches Tillerson. He is calm and polite. "Please take your position on the floor with your friends."

"I will not! I demand to speak to your Supervisor."

The pleasant plain-clothes pseudo cop hits Tillerson in the face knocking him backwards. He goes down with a thud, his head bouncing off the carpeted floor. The two uniformed cops tell everyone to get up and move to the lounge room. "Not you Rothman, you take a seat on the couch." Rothman does exactly as he's told; he understands these men aren't cops. There is no sense putting up a fuss. What's about to happen will happen.

The other plain-clothes cop grabs Tillerson lifting him by the scruff of the neck off the floor and deposits him on the couch beside Rothman. Tillerson is conscious but groggy; Rothman is quiet. He's a professional. He knows what's probably in store for him, and he's resigned to the inevitable. He thinks maybe they won't kill him; maybe if he's lucky, they'll just beat him half to death. Whatever they do, he gets it. It's a fact of life, and it's the life he's chosen.

The leader of the cops speaks. He's still calm and polite. "Mr. Tillerson can you hear me?"

"You fucking hit me!"

"And I'll hit you again if you don't start co-operating. So what's it going to be? Listen and co-operate, or we break your arms, making it difficult for you to jerk off." The other plain-clothes cop taps his watch signaling time is running out.

"Mr. Tillerson, please listen carefully. Here is what you are going to do. You're going to call a board meeting and announce the resignation of Clarkson, Taylor, McDonald, and Trembly. You are then going to appoint Stanley Yufu, Zack Wei, Milton Goldstein, and Jesse James as new board members."

"What if those board members don't want to resign?"

"Oh they'll want to resign all right. And here's why. They are currently being given the same opportunity to have the use of their arms and legs as we have offered you. And if for some reason they fail to resign, well, there are always other more extreme remedies. So are we clear?"

"Yes, perfectly."

"Fine. I'm glad we've been able to resolve this matter to everyone's satisfaction. Mr. Tillerson, please go into the other room and join your friends." The cop turns to his partner, "Keep an eye on Rothman." He follows Tillerson into the lounge. The two uniformed cops and Mai Ling are standing guard. Everyone else is facedown on the floor with their hands on their heads. Tillerson joins them.

"I want everyone to stay exactly where you are for the next hour, at which time you may stay and continue your game, or you may leave. We are taking your phones, but leaving your money and wallets, this is not a robbery. In fact this has nothing to do with any of you so we advise you to mind your own business.

If anyone decides to go the authorities in an hour,
a day, or a year, we'll find you and kill you. It's
that simple. And if you really feel strongly about
telling someone about this little party, I suggest
you think of your family's welfare. You wouldn't
want anything bad to happen to them."

Some brave soul asks, "How do we know when
it's an hour?"

"You'll know. When you here the alarm it will be
an hour." He places an egg time on the coffee
table and sets it for an hour. One of the cops
takes a cloth and wipes down any surface the
four intruders touched.

The four pseudo policemen, Mai Ling, and Morris
Rothman leave. They go directly to a service
elevator where one of their Lion Dog men
dressed in a hotel uniform is waiting. They
proceed down to the lowest parking level and get
into two waiting SUVs.

At about four-thirty in the morning one of the SUVs pulls up to the emergency entrance of the Mount Sinai Hospital. The back door of the SUV opens and Morris Rothman's badly beaten body is pushed out onto the pavement. His association with Albert The Artist Giacometti has been terminated. In future, after a long and painful recuperation period he will be allowed to continue his operation under the supervision and for the benefit of the Hong Mian and Fungi Family alliance.

THE SOKOLOVS KILL TIME

20.
The Sokolovs Kill Time

Sasha and Simcha Sokolov are shadowed twenty-four hours a day by a team of revolving Lion Dog Club members. Wei wasn't taking any chances that the two Russian-Israeli assassins would decide to fulfill their contract on Jesse. Wei liked Jesse and wouldn't want to see anything nasty happen to her, besides, if something bad did happen on his watch, Johnny Luck would be sure to come down hard on the poor souls that were supposed to be protecting her.

It would only be another day and they'd be off to Italy to put an end to the legend of Albert The Artist Giacometti. How they did it is up to them, perhaps a bullet in the back of the head at a restaurant urinal from Simcha, or a spiked drink at a bar from Sasha, it really didn't matter, as long as the job got done. It was better no one but the Sokolovs knew the details, just in case things went wrong.

Jesse looked out her office window that overlooked the track. Sasha and Simcha were sitting in the grandstand watching the early morning exercise riders. Their Lion Dog keepers were sitting about eight rows back relaxing. Simcha was playing with one of those camera drones you can buy in any electronic shop or camera store.

Jesse thought to herself, 'everybody's got to have a hobby, even murders. Perhaps she should take up something, something physical, maybe Squash.' The thought of physical activity made her think, 'Jesus… its been a long time since I got laid. Too much time spent around horses and hoodlums.' She decides sex is something to be added to her to-do list, yes sex and Squash, maybe there's a way she can combine the two to save time.

Her musings are interrupted by the drone appearing in the window directly in front of her. She sees the shutter snap. "What the hell do those two clowns think they're playing at? No fucking pictures."

Jesse stomps out of her office and heads down to the grandstand. When she gets there, she sees Simcha has the drone hovering high above the starting gate. A couple of horses break out of the gate, the drone drops down behind them. It has no trouble keeping up with the horses. Once the horses complete their workout, Simcha flies the drone back to where he and his partner are sitting. The drone lands in the aisle beside Simcha.

Jesse approaches. "That thing is fast."

Sasha and Simcha turn to see who it is. "Yeah… this model can hit about fifty miles-an-hour and has a range of about seven kilometers."

"I guess everybody has to have a hobby."

Simcha picks up the drone and makes a few adjustments. "Sure, you could say that. It's fun, you should try it."

Jesse thinks for a minute, "How much did that thing cost?"

Simcha looks at Sasha, Sasha answers, "Just under sixteen hundred Canadian."

"Can I see it?"

Simcha hands Jesse the drone. Jesse looks at it as if she's really interested. "Nice... expensive, but nice." Jesse drops the drone on hard concrete step in front of her; then stomps on it with the heel of her boot. She picks up the camera's SIM card from the pile of broken plastic and electronic parts.

Simcha doesn't react, but Sasha looks pissed. "That was our property."

Jesse bends down eyeball to eyeball with Sasha. She appears calm, but underneath she's seething. "It was your property; now it's your garbage. You ever try to take a picture of me again and I'll slit your throats while you sleep. And if you ever fly that stupid fucking toy over my track again, I'll see you end up at the bottom of Lake Erie. You could have spooked those horse and caused an accident. This isn't your fucking playground, go find someplace else to cause trouble."

Jesse turns around to the two smiling Lion Dog chaperons who are sitting a few rows back enjoying the dressing down of the two killers. "What, the fuck, are you two numskulls smiling about? Get these two dummies the hell off my race track."

MEMENTO MORI PART ONE
TILLERSON'S LINCOLN MOMENT

21.
Memento Mori Part One
Tillerson's Lincoln Moment

Taking over the board of the Woodbridge Downs Racing & Entertainment Complex went smoothly. None of the wealthy, horsey Rosedale and Bridal Path types wanted any trouble. No one wanted to end up in the trunk of a car at the airport.

Tillerson was left ostensibly in charge, but in truth his position was strictly ceremonial. He presented awards, had his picture taken with celebrities, and went to dinner parties and government functions representing the track and casino.

The Crystal Beach track, laundering, drug businesses were running smoothly, so Johnny Luck sent in new people from the Hancock operation in LA to take over running the place. Jesse was put in charge of the Woodbridge track venture, Goldstein was appointed the comptroller, and Zack Wei was made head of security. Nicky Fungo's people took over the casino.

Tillerson had no idea what was going on with regards to the ecstasy smuggling business. He wisely chose to close his eyes to the money-laundering scheme Jesse installed, but when it came to Fungo's men overrunning the casino, Tillerson squawked. He was afraid the government would make a stink despite the fact none of Fungo's casino people had records; they were just people who knew people, who were friends of the people who counted.

As long as the government was raking in the dough from the various racetracks and casinos they didn't care who was running things. Benson Yeung could dig up Myer Lansky and put him in charge, and they wouldn't say a word as long as nobody opened their big mouth; but Tillerson wouldn't shut up about the "cuff-shooting Italians in their chalk-stripped suits and imported tassel loafers." He kept yapping about the hoodlum element running his casino; wondering out loud how much they were skimming.

His Angelo Saxon prejudice didn't confine itself to the swarthy Italian menace; his narrow-minded contempt for anyone whose pappy wasn't a United Empire Loyalist extended to the Chinese thugs operating the track. Jesse didn't escape Tillerson's broad brush of condescension. He regarded her as just some trailer park bitch with a foul mouth that had to be fucking somebody to get where she was. If Tillerson wasn't muzzled soon, the news media might get interested, and that could potentially bring down the whole house of cards. It was time for Eddy Tillerson to retire.

Toronto has a lively theatre district with the Royal Alexandra Theatre, more commonly referred to as the Royal Alex, arguably its crown jewel. Completed in 1907 in the style of 19th century British theatres, it is both aesthetically pleasing in its turn of the century red velvet dress, and totally comfortable for each and every of one of the just under fifteen hundred people that cram into the place every Saturday evening. The theatre is named after Queen Alexandra, the Danish princess married to King Edward VII. The theatre received letters of patent from the monarch bestowing on it the royal designation, most likely the only remaining "royal theatre" in North America.

Sitting in the second balcony, stage left is Edward P. Tillerson III and his wife Margaret, a middle-aged, anorexic blonde, trying her damnedest to pass for twenty years younger than she could comfortably pull off. Seated in the other two chairs are Tillerson's lawyer and his wife. Standing behind them at the door to the private box is a young Page ready to cater to the two society-couples every need. Tonight's performance was a Shakespearean revival of King Lear staged in an urban city setting... Shakespeare is likely rolling over in his grave. Everything seemed normal for the packed house of Saturday night theater goers.

The regular Page that normally commands the stage-left upper private box suddenly came down with a severe case of Nicky Fungoitis. Nicky's wife's second cousin once removed was drafted to take his place. The young man is given instructions to offer his charges a cocktail, with Edward Tillerson's drink specially concocted with an overdose of Molly and an added pinch of fentanyl stirred in for good measure.

Near the end of the play Tillerson starts to sweat, his mouth is dry, his vision is blurred, and he starts hallucinating. He lurches to his feet, turns to his wife, and vomits all over her Vera Wang original. She swears, instinctively pushing him away. He stumbles backwards tripping over the ornate heavy velvet and mahogany Victorian theater chair banging hard into the balcony railing that somehow gives way due to the Pages foresight to loosen the screws holding the brass protective barrier in place. Tillerson hits the railing and goes over, falling thirty feet to the stage below. He lands with a bang.

The actors stop, they are unsure of what has just happened, the audience gasps in surprise, some applaud thinking it's part of the play, then Mrs. Tillerson screams.

Panic ensures the theatre becomes a scene of bedlam with people rushing in every direction; some imagining a terror attack head for the exits while others rush to the stage to try to help. The lawyer and his wife turn to the Page, but he's long gone. Edward P. Tillerson III is retired, permanently, for not keeping his big mouth shut.

**MEMENTO MORI PART TWO
GIACOMETTI'S CALABRESE RETREAT**

22.
Memento Mori Part Two
Giacometti's Calabrese Retreat

Giacometti's Scilla Cliff Side Villa is something out of a James Bond movie. The stone villa with a terracotta tiled roof is a classic Italian seaside country house. The terraced veranda perched on a rocky cliff side overlooks the Strait of Messina with a perfect view of the Aeolian Islands. Scilla is a picturesque fishing village. Everyone knows the villa belongs to the American Mafioso.

He shows up with his two French mistresses several times a year and strolls through the village like he owns the place, which is okay with the locals as long as he keeps leaving large tips everywhere he goes. People bow as he walks by, but if they get too friendly, one of his two ever-present bodyguards steps in.

A thick forest of trees and bushes surrounds the villa guarding access. The only way in to the villa is from the narrow winding road that wraps around the mini mountain to the properties electrocuted front gate, manned by an armed member of Giacometti's crew. Access from the sea is made impossible by the treacherous formation of giant rocks that stand guard in the water at the bottom of the property the locals call *Il Posto Del Padrino*, The Godfather's Place.

About seven kilometers anchored out in the Strait of Messina is a rented luxury outboard with the beautiful Sasha Sokolov sunning herself on the bow like an exotic ornamental pirate figurehead. Simcha sits on the floor of the deck with a disassembled camera drone that he is rewiring so the camera triggers a small brick of C4 explosives. Jesse was wrong; Simcha's interest in drones was purely professional; he had no hobbies other than Sasha. She joins Simcha under the protection of the boat's canopy.

On shore about seven kilometers from *Il Posto Del Padrino*, Mo Fields lies prostrate on a rock that overhangs the Strait of Messina. He looks through the scope of his powerful long-range sniper's rifle left on the pillow of his hotel room bed beside a box of ammunition and a delicious Italian chocolate. He should have saved the chocolate for his daughter Betty, but he ate it. Perhaps he'd pick some up in the village and take them home, maybe even buy some for Johnny Luck and Benson Yeung. No, that would be a mistake, no souvenirs, no evidence.

He moves the rife around until he sees Giacometti enjoying his morning coffee. He moves the scope to check out the two French women who are all but naked except for the piece of string that passes for a bikini bottom. He then repositions himself so he has a direct line of sight to Sasha and Simcha Sokolov.

On shore, two of Giacometti's men stand guard to the entrance of the terraced patio. The two French mistresses sun themselves in their matching white string bikinis. Giacometti sits at the table wearing a thin cotton robe and boxer shorts, enjoying a substantial brunch prepared by his cook, the wife of a local restaurant owner. The day is beautiful. The scene is beautiful. The French mistresses are beautiful. Life is good for Albert The Artist Giacometti.

The Sun is getting too strong for the delicate French beauties so they decide to go inside to take a shower and dress for the ritual afternoon walk around the village. The women kiss Giacometti on either cheek and disappear into the villa. As Giacometti reaches for his orange juice, Simcha Sokolov's camera drone drops down in front of him hovering at eye level, just out of reach. Giacometti drops his orange juice. There is a faint click, then BOOM!

Mo Fields adjusts the rife focusing on Simcha Sokolov raising the anchor of the outboard. He fires. The bullet rips through the forehead of the Russian-Israeli hitman. He falls into the Strait of Messina. Sasha panics. She races to start the engine to make her escape. She presses the starter just as Fields fires. The bullet enters the back of Sasha's head and exits ending up in the deck of the boat. The boat races away from the scene out to sea with a dead Sasha Sokolov draped over the steering wheel.

TRUFFATORE'S CHINESE DINNER

23.
Truffatore's Chinese Dinner

Tony Truffatore enters the Rose Garden Chinese Eatery. The place is not your usual Buffalo Chop Suey joint; it's an elegant high-class restaurant that caters to Buffalo's more colorful characters, people like Nicky The Mushroom Fungo.

Truffatore is a horse trainer, but not just any horse trainer, a trainer with three ex-wives, a bunch of kids in private schools, and a gambling problem that sometimes makes him useful to Nicky Fungo. If you owe Nicky money and he tells you to be at the Rose Garden at nine o'clock on Saturday, you show up. You never know if the meeting will result in a favor or a beating. So far Truffatore has been lucky. The last time was in Florida, hopefully this time it will be more of the same.

An attractive Chinese hostess approaches. She's wearing a skintight ankle length black silk cheongsam with a slit up the side. A gold embroidered dragon plunges from the high standup collar down over her chest covering her abdomen and across her hip. Her long lustrous jet-black hair is held in place by a gold lacquer *ji* pin. The only other decoration on the dress is an 18k gold Guan Yu pin on the collar of her dress. She is by all reckoning, stunning. Truffatore stares. She ignores the visual undressing, she's used to it. "Table for one?"

"I'm here to meet Mr. Fungo."

The hostess snaps her fingers signaling another exotic beauty to take over her station. The action is one of authority and not just a glorified hourly waitress.

Truffatore looks closer. The woman could pass for thirty but she is older than she looks; the telltale signs of age have just barely started to impinge on her exotic looks. She's not the hostess; she's Miss Zhan, owner of the Rose Garden Chinese Eatery and the leading Madame in Western New York.

"Follow me, please?" It's polite, but an order nonetheless.

He follows Miss Zhan, watching the black silk enjoying its position of envy as it makes its way through the dark lit, not quite bohemian, atmosphere drenched in black lacquer and gold silk. In the background you can hear a recording of Jasmine Chen singing her version of Dave Brubeck's *Take Five* in Cantonese. Miss Z, as she is known, takes Truffatore through the kitchen where a variety of cooks work diligently in almost militaristic lockstep.

They go through a small door, down a set of rickety wooden steps, Truffatore marvels at the woman's ability to maneuver the uneven stairs in her six inch spiked heels that turn her petit five foot two frame into a more intimidating five foot eight. They work their way through a well-stocked wine cellar and a room filled with chairs and tables that have obviously been retired from service.

They finally reach a private dining room with a round table that could accommodate about twelve people. The room is poorly lit on purpose. The walls are painted in a shiny black acrylic paint. A golden dragon stretches across the entire back wall.

Sitting at the table is Nicky Fungo; Johnny Luck sits on Nicky's left while Jesse James occupies the seat on his right. Truffatore knows Luck and Jesse from his time in LA working at the Hancock Race Track for one of his clients, Mrs. Murphy. Murphy, the beneficiary of her late husband's fortune made by spreading peanut butter across a nation that never saw a calorie it didn't like, was not one of Johnny Luck's or Jesse James' favorite people.

Miss Z bows to her seated guests and signals Truffatore to sit in a chair opposite Nicky Fungo. Nicky thanks Miss Z in Chinese, "*Xiexie*... please bring my friend an order of *Mianyang de yinjing*."

Miss Z bows and leaves. Truffatore asks, "Don't think I ever had that, what is it?"

Nicky takes a drink of wine, looks Truffatore in the eye, and responds, "Sheep's penis… I think you'll like the way they do it here." Truffatore throws-up a little in his mouth. He swallows small bits of upchuck imaging what a sheep's penis tastes like. He doesn't dare object.

"You still work for that Murphy woman?"

"Sure, sure, she's running a few horses next week in Florida. In fact I'm leaving tomorrow for Hallandale."

"I need you to do me a little favor."

"You know I'd do anything for you, Nicky, but I got eyes on me. I'm just coming off a suspension, and they'll be all over me like soy on rice." Miss Z drops a plate of three fried skewered sheep's penises in front of Truffatore. Tony looks at the plate and then at Miss Z. She smiles, "*Qing xiangyong*… enjoy." She winks at Nicky and leaves.

"It's easy, you won't get in any trouble."

"Yeah but they'll be watching me like a hawk."

Fungo leans forward, "Try your *Mianyang de yinjing*."

"You know I just ate before I came. Really, I'm stuffed."

Fungo leans further across the table, picks up one of the skewers and shoves it in Truffatore's mouth. "I said I need a favor, and people who owe me money just don't say no, otherwise they might be chewing on their own *Yinjing... Capice!*"

Truffatore mumbles something that sounds like a "Yes" but with a mouth full of sheep's penis it's hard to tell. Fungo turns to Jesse, "What did he say? Jesse shrugs her shoulders.

Truffatore takes the skewer out of his mouth gagging as he swallows a small bit of animal private parts.

Fungo gives him a hard look, "Don't you throw up. Don't you fucking, dare, throw up! You upchuck in here and Miss Z will cut your heart out and serve it to her dog. Then you won't be able to do me that favor."

"Okay, okay... I was just saying people are watching me, but I'll do whatever you want. What do you want me to do?"

"Murphy's got a filly... Trojan Surprise."

"Yeah that's right, she's a rabbit, doesn't like to run from the back, hates getting hit with all the mud."

"Perfect... I want you to have Doc Simons check her out."

"It's not necessary, I just had her checked over before I sent her to Florida."

"You know Tony... you got a problem, you don't fucking listen. I want you to have Simons check her out – in private, understand. That's all you have to do... Oh yeah, you need to make sure AJ Gonzalez is the jockey."

"You want AJ on Trojan Surprise, sure why not?"

"One more thing..." Fungo slides a small box across the table. "Give this to Doc Simons."

Truffatore lifts the lid of the box revealing a medium brown brick of what could have been plasticine but isn't, "Is that what I think it is?"

Fungo smiles, "You really want me to tell you?"

"But..."

"But nothing! Just do it. Do it without causing me any more aggravation and I'll knock ten grand off what you owe me."

"Sure Nicky, consider it done." Truffatore gets up to leave.

"Where are you going? You haven't finished your *Mianyang de yinjing*."

**MEMENTO MORI PART THREE
THE TROJAN SURPRISE**

24.
Memento Mori Part Three
The Trojan Surprise

The Hallandale Park Clubhouse is a beautiful half circle of Spanish Colonial Revival complete with curves and arches topped with a terracotta tile roof that houses the casino and fronts the entrance to the grandstand and pari-mutuel windows.

The facility was built in 1939 by a group of Yankee bankers that liked the ponies and the real estate potential of the area. The one-and-an-eighth dirt course surrounds a one-mile turf course that surrounds a huge artificial lake populated by a family of white and black swans. As Jesse enters the clubhouse, she thinks maybe she should talk to Johnny about targeting Hallandale as their next object of opportunity.

Jesse is wearing a black wig, oversized Hollywood starlet sunglasses, and a big floppy hat. The place is full of cameras and it would be unwise to be too easily identified. She entered the country on a fake passport provided by Stanley Yufu. For the next day or so, she was Dorothy Sales from Kingston, Ontario, a part-time office worker looking for some sun and fun. She wasn't used to wearing a dress, and the high heels left no room for her pearl-handled switchblade. She felt naked.

She spots Doc Simons in the snack bar eating a white bread sandwich of ham and cheese, nursing a large mug of coffee. She approaches Simons who doesn't recognize her at first. "How's the food here?"

"Not bad… Jesse? Is that you? Didn't know you had such nice legs."

"Good eye Doc. I'm full of surprises once you get to know me."

"I'll bet."

"Is it done?"

"Of course, no problem. Not quite your usual Caslick, but the girl is fully loaded."

"You going to hang around for the show?"

"Are you crazy? I'm on a plane to Argentina in an hour. I have a client down there that's been after me for months to come check out his horses. Besides, I don't want to be anywhere near this place in an hour."

"You take care Doc… see you on the other side."

"Be careful Jesse, the walls have eyes."

Jesse nods and heads for the snack bar to get something to eat. She orders a Club Sandwich and Diet Coke. She finishes downing her lunch without much regard to how it tastes. She's too ramped up.

She looks up at the in-house race monitors hanging from the ceiling in the snack bar and sees the end of the sixth race. She makes her way to the betting windows where she buys a ten-dollar ticket on Number 5 in the seventh race without even looking at the name of the horse or the odds. She figures she needs to bet on more than one race, otherwise it might look fishy to anyone that investigates, and there sure as hell will be an investigation.

She buys another ticket on Number 5, in the eight-race, Trojan Surprise. She heads to the grandstand and finds a vacant seat amongst a group of enthusiastic racing fans. The best way to remain anonymous is to hide in plain sight. She takes a seat and waits. The seventh race is about to start. She casually checks out the Number 5 horse, a beautiful jet-black beauty with white stockings. She's curious to find out about the horse she's bet on.

She turns to the man sitting beside her. "Can I borrow your program for a minute?" The man hands her his program. Number 5 is a forty-to-one long shot called Last Chance. Jesse hands the man back his program.

The horses come out of the gate with Last Chance last. Jesse figures she can kiss her ten bucks goodbye. The horses make their way around the far turn and into the backstretch. Last Chance has moved up to fifth place. They come around the Clubhouse turn and Last Chance is holding in fifth. As the horses pass the three-sixteenth pole, Last Chance makes its move. People are cheering and Jesse finds herself on her feet screaming at the jockey, "Go to the whip! For Christ sake, go to the whip!" The man who leant Jesse the program turns and smiles. They hit the wire and Last Chance wins by half a length. The man beside Jesse rips up his ticket. He turns to Jesse, "How'd you do?"

Jesse doesn't want to be remembered, so she lies, "About the same as you."

He shakes his head, "Damn long shots, go figure that dog would win."

Jesse commiserates, "Yeah… go figure."

Jesse feels she's talked enough to this guy and heads back inside to cash her ticket and get lost in the crowd. She'll find some place else to watch the next race. She kills some time checking out the facilities ultimately making her way to the balcony of the grandstand where she positions herself between the three-sixteenth pole and the one-eighth pole.

She takes out her burner phone provided by Zack Wei especially for this occasion. Jesse has memorized the number. Putting the number in the phone would be sloppy. Everything was thought-out. No evidence. No loose ends. No mistakes.

She made the call on Lucy Chao but this was different, this was hands-on. It started out as simple revenge. AJ tried to kill her on the track. She still felt the aches and pains from her injuries when the weather was cold and damp. All she was doing was returning the favor; only she wouldn't fail.

But this had become something more, more than revenge. She's a woman, not much more than a girl in a man's world where soft gets eaten alive. This is about crossing the proverbial Rubicon: proving to Johnny, Benson, Yufu, and Wei, that she is one of them. Even Nicky Fungo would have to be impressed. Nobody... fucking nobody could deny this bitch has balls!

The horses are loaded into the gates without any problems. Her racing instincts flood her brain with the memories of her riding days. She can practically feel Trojan Surprise pushing her rump back against the gate ready to propel herself forward. She likes taking the lead, getting pounded with rock hard dirt is just not in her DNA. She anticipates the almost inaudible electronic gate release; her ears react to the silent secret message, and the gates fly open.

Trojan Surprise propels herself forward. There's some initial jostling and bumping. The six-horse comes out crooked banging into Trojan Surprise knocking her into the four-horse. She stumbles, righting herself almost immediately, but she's last.

Jesse doesn't care if she's dead last or ahead by a mile, as long as she doesn't get caught in the pack. AJ goes to the whip almost immediately, he always was a prick, but there's no denying he knows how to ride. They get to the first turn and Trojan Surprise has caught up to the pack and made her way into sixth place. She's getting pummeled by the dirt and starts to drop back. AJ takes her to the outside as they enter the backstretch. He's driving her hard, too hard. Jesse thinks he's killing her, not realizing she's about to do the same.

Trojan Surprise is third as they make the turn for home. Jesse dials the number on the phone leaving the last number for the last second. This is going to be messy, she could kill half the field, she hesitates… maybe she doesn't have the guts; maybe she doesn't have what it takes?

AJ goes to the whip again. Trojan Surprise sees daylight and the finish line. She gives it everything she's got. She separates herself from the pack. She hits the eighth pole with a two-length lead; at the sixteenth pole it's four lengths. Jesse dials the last number… BOOM!

Jesse can't look. She turns and starts walking. She did it. She made her bones. She's crossed the line to the other side. There is no turning back. As she leaves the grounds, she sees a city garbage bin. She wipes down the phone with a tissue, removes the SIM card, and drops the phone in the bin. She'll dispose of the SIM card in a roadside sewer drain somewhere else. She's not just Johnny Luck's prized pupil anymore; she's Jesse fucking James, gangster bitch, ready to take her place at the table with the big boys.

THE END

Author Biography

Jerry Bader is Senior Partner at MRPwebmedia.com, a media production company that specializes in Web video, audio, music, and sound design. Mr. Bader has written and produced dozens of video commercials for clients. Writing scripts and novels is a natural extension that grew out of the experience of creating attention-grabbing mini movies that focus on the core emotional motivator.

Over the years Mr. Bader has written over a hundred articles on marketing, and he's self-published marketing e-books, hybrid graphic novels, biographies, and a series of children's books. The Neo Noir Hybrid Graphic Novels are story concepts developed with the goal of having them turned into television series or feature films. There are currently ten screenplays, five of which have been self-published as hybrid graphic novels: *The Method, The Comeuppance, The Coffin Corner, Grist For The Mill* and *The Black Crane.*

He's also written *The Fixer* published by Rebel Seed Entertainment. It has consistently been in the top ten percent in several Amazon categories. *The Fixer* is based on the true-life story of a colorful horse racing character. The follow-up to *The Fixer* is the new book *Beating The System* that continues the story of the horse racing legend. Mr. Bader has also written *Organized Crime Queens, The Secret World of Female Gangsters, What's Your Poison? How Cocktails Got Their Names, Cowboys, Lawmen, and Outlaws, The Outlaw Rider, Dead End, and the soon to be released: Palermo, Stone Cold, The Aussie Switch,* and *Ballet Of Bullets.*

Mr. Bader has also written a series of children's books, ZaZa Books For Kids, that currently includes, *Two Dragons Named Shoe, The Town That Didn't Speak, The Criminal McBride, The Bad Puppeteer, Mr. Bumbershoot, The Umbrella Man, The Ninth Inning,* and *14 Ridiculous Tales of Sage Silliness.*

The Outlaw Rider

THE OUTLAW RIDER

BEATING THE SYSTEM

NOIR I
JERRY BADER
THE GOLD CRICKET
THE BASTARD
CINE CITY
KILLER JAZZ

NOIR I

NOIR II
JERRY BADER
CULT
THE RED EMPEROR
THE REDHEAD RIP-OFF
THE INCIDENT REPORT

NOIR II

WHAT'S YOUR POISON?